GRIM DISCOVERY

"Danica?" Jamie approached Danica's bedroom door, which was slightly ajar and located at the end of a short, narrow hallway with dark-paneled walls and a dingy linoleum floor that creaked under her footsteps.

At the end of the hallway Jamie stopped, taking note of the fact that her palms were sweaty, her heart was thumping unusually fast, and there was a queasy feeling in the pit of her stomach. All symptoms of fear. She told herself firmly that there was no reason for her to be afraid. Danica was behind that door with speaker plugs in her ears while she doodled her and Roman's initials inside hearts. Or she wasn't here at all. Danica had too much on her mind to worry about whether or not she'd locked the front door.

Pasting a smile on her face, Jamie pushed Danica's bedroom door open.

For a moment the sight that greeted her was too horrible to be believed. The smile she'd pasted on wilted instantly, but the rest of her body remained frozen in place. Then the truth slammed home and Jamie fell back into the hallway, releasing a bloodcurdling scream.

THE NIGHT OWL CLUB
IT'S COOL—
IT'S FUN—
IT'S TERRIFYING—
AND YOU CAN JOIN IT . . . IF YOU DARE!

Scream

#1: BLOOD PACT

Debra Franklin

Z·FAVE
KENSINGTON PUBLISHING CORP.

Z*FAVE BOOKS are published by

Kensington Publishing Corp.
475 Park Avenue South
New York, NY 10016

First Printing: September, 1993

Printed in the United States of America

Chapter One

His lips were getting closer. Jon Bon Jovi was about to plant an earthshaking kiss on her waiting mouth, which would undoubtedly transport her into an eternal state of bliss.

Then the telephone rang and woke her up. Jamie hated it when that happened.

Groping for the offending instrument on her nightstand, she hoped that whoever had cheated her out of such an excellent experience, even if it was just a dream (like she'd been aware of that minor detail until the stupid phone rang) would suffer the most hideous pimple breakout ever seen.

After mumbling a disgruntled hello into the mouthpiece, Jamie's left eardrum came under assault by the voice of her best friend, Danica Hooker, whose Oklahoma twang immediately began blaring loudly and shrilly through the receiver, her words so jumbled and run together that Jamie could hardly understand a thing she was saying. Something about the newspaper.

Wincing, Jamie jerked the phone away and

stuffed it under her pillow, sighed and silently counted out ten seconds (one *why me?*, two *why me?*) which she assumed would be long enough for Danica to run out of steam. Her timing had been correct. When she retrieved the instrument from under her pillow, Danica's voice had lost its hysterical edge and was now inquiring, "Jamie, are you there? Did you go back to sleep? Jamie . . . ?"

Jamie groaned, stretching. "Danica, it's only eight-thirty. You know I like to sleep till noon on Saturdays, and you interrupted a really fantastic dream. I was just about to kiss—"

"But didn't you hear me?" Danica interrupted, her voice raising an octave. "Mayor Shepherd's going to tear down the old railroad depot and put in some stupid memorial statue and flower gardens with benches. And the demolition starts Monday after next!"

It took a few moments for the message to sink into Jamie's muddled brain, but when it did, she was jolted into full alertness. "Are you *serious?*" Springing upright, she tossed back a long tangle of her strawberry blond hair, which presently looked like a bird's nest.

"Go take a look at this morning's *Review;* it's right on the front page next to the article about Emma Parker breaking her leg." In a town of only thirty-five hundred such as Deer Creek, broken legs and just about everything else including disastrous home permanents were newsworthy.

Jamie was stunned. She, along with every other teenager in Deer Creek, felt a deep attachment to

6

the abandoned railroad depot on the northwest side of town. It was and always had been their favorite hangout, a tradition handed down by their parents. Admittedly the dilapidated building was an eyesore even though it bore a fairly recent coat of red paint, but Jamie couldn't believe the mayor would even think of tearing it down. That old depot was as much an integral part of Deer Creek as the Town Hall, which wasn't exactly Caesar's Palace.

"We need to get together with the guys and talk about this," she said with an uncharacteristic note of determination. Jamie Fox was typically mellow (spelled *l-a-z-y* by her achievement-oriented father), not easily rattled by the winds of adversity—or Ds on her report card, like she by-God ought to be—but Danica's news riled her considerably. There had to be some way to keep the mayor from carrying out his plan.

"What's there to talk about?" Danica responded sulkily. "We can't stop the mayor. Teenagers don't have a voice in this stinkhole of a town."

"But we can't just sit back and watch it happen. We've at least got to try," Jamie insisted. "Listen, I'll pick you up in an hour. Call the guys and tell them to meet us at the depot."

"What am I, your secretary?"

Jamie expelled a heavy sigh into the mouthpiece, throwing her horrendous morning swamp breath back up at her. She winced. "Okay, you call Alan and Roman and I'll call Keith. Now g'bye." She depressed the cutoff button before Danica could think of any more testy comebacks. A few seconds later when she was rewarded with a dial tone, she started dialing Keith's number, but stopped midway and replaced the receiver in its aqua cradle. First she'd shower, brush her teeth, and get dressed, then she would call Keith. That was just in case he had psychic powers he hadn't told anyone about, and that by listening to her voice he could receive an image of her, see what a wreck she was, sitting there wearing her dorkiest pair of pajamas. It was really a dumb notion and Keith was just a friend, but Jamie headed for the bathroom in the upstairs hallway anyway.

After showering and putting herself together, Jamie headed downstairs for breakfast. As she bounced into the kitchen she saw her mother looking up from the dining table in surprise, which was understandable, considering it was only nine-fifteen. It was common knowledge in the Fox household that Jamie always slept late on the weekends, and that for at least an hour after getting up she would drag herself around like a heavy sack of potatoes. If she did any bouncing, it would be off a doorjamb or wall because she wasn't paying enough attention to where she was going.

Yet here she was up and dressed three hours earlier than usual for a Saturday and exuding an uncharacteristic amount of energy. Jamie could see a faint alarm going off in her mother's eyes.

"Something special going on, dear?" Gloria Fox

asked casually.

Wanting to put her mother's fears that she was up to something sneaky to a rest, Jamie stalked up to the table and jabbed a finger at the newspaper, folded to the crossword section, her mother was holding. "Didn't you read what Mayor Shepherd plans to do to the old depot? Danica said the story was on the front page."

Her mother reflected a moment, during which her eyes took on a distant look, then she exclaimed with a smile, "Oh! That. Yes, well, the building's so old it's getting to be a danger, dear. Never know when it might decide to collapse, and someone— you, for instance—could get hurt. I think the flower gardens would be much better, don't you?"

Jamie was no longer a gullible child willing to accept any explanation given to her. She'd done some thinking in the shower, and she was pretty sure she'd figured out the motivation behind Shepherd's plan. He was coming up for reelection pretty soon, and this time he had a contender, Malcolm Monroe. Monroe had lived in the area only a few years, but he'd brought a couple of businesses with him, businesses that had substantially improved Deer Creek's meager economy.

Monroe's son, Morey, attended her high school and he was in a number of classes with her. He was a major hunk who was popular with practically everyone in the school, especially the girls. Jamie was also no exception to his dark good looks, and on more than one occasion, especially during a boring class, she had found herself wondering what it would be like to go out with him. Probably all she would ever do was wonder. Morey tended to have a new girlfriend almost every month and he seemed to date only the most popular girls in school, especially those on the cheerleading squad. If there was one thing Jamie *wasn't,* or ever intended to be, it was cheerleading material. It was Morey's loss!

Gene Shepherd had been mayor of Deer Creek for twelve years, and he was very fond of the position. He would use every trick in the book and make up some new ones if necessary, whatever it took to hold his ground. Tearing down the depot and erecting a scene out of Camelot was simply part of his reelection strategy.

"It's not as shaky as it looks, and anyway you said that was where Dad proposed to you. It wouldn't bother you at all to see it torn down?"

A gentle smile emerged on Gloria's pale, careworn face. "I know how you feel, Jamie, but please, don't do anything that would embarrass your father. He's still hasn't quite gotten over that incident with Miss Frupp."

Miss Frupp was the secondary school's English teacher, and she had given Jamie an F on her essay titled "Small Towns/Small Minds," which Jamie had actually worked very hard on, at least by her standards. At any rate Jamie, and her friends, were of the opinion that the F was totally undeserved, but Miss Frupp had refused to even discuss the issue, much less change the grade. Jamie had then casually mentioned to Keith (who lived a few miles

10

from town on a dairy farm) how fitting it would be if someone brought a stale cow pie to school and placed it in the seat of Miss Frupp's chair. Oddly enough someone had done just that the very next day, and it had gone unnoticed by Miss Frupp until she sat down. Of course, by that evening every living soul in Deer Creek had heard the story. The old-timers who spent most of their empty hours in Ruby's Lounge thought it was a real hoot, and the juvenile set took great delight for weeks in imitating Miss Frupp's expression during the moment of truth. Her father, however, had not been the least bit amused.

"What do you think I'm going to do, Mom? Chain myself to one of the depot's support pillars?"

"Oh, *heavens*." Gloria Fox put a well-manicured hand to her collarbone. In the bright morning light pouring through the kitchen curtains, she looked every day of her thirty-eight years, a faded beauty queen with dark red hair and nothing much to do anymore except bake cookies for the church bazaars. "Jamie, don't even joke about doing such a thing, especially around your friends. One of them might think it was a good idea."

That was true; in fact, it was right up Keith's alley. Jamie could also picture him dressed in an army battle-dress uniform, warding off approaching bulldozers with rotten egg missiles. "Don't worry, Mom. I was thinking more in the direction of a protest letter. That's allowable, isn't it? It is according to the Constitution, anyway."

Jamie smiled to herself, knowing that her mother could hardly argue against Constitutional rights. Her father probably would, but thankfully she wasn't dealing with him. Yet.

Gloria acknowledged defeat with a long sigh. "Would you like some bacon and eggs?"

"No time," Jamie said, turning to pull an unripe banana from the bunch sitting on the kitchen counter. "I'll just eat this on my way to Danica's. I told her I'd be there at nine-thirty."

"That banana's not much of a breakfast."

"I'm not very hungry," Jamie called back on her way out, leaving her mother sitting at the table shaking her head, a worried expression etched into her once-beautiful face.

Alan, Roman, and Keith had been waiting at the depot for almost twenty minutes by the time Jamie and Danica arrived in Jamie's new Corsica, which her father had gone to Elk City to buy. If you wanted to buy a vehicle in Deer Creek, you'd best be wanting a pickup, jeep, or tractor.

"Sorry we're late," Jamie apologized as she stepped onto the wide sagging porch where Keith and Roman were engaged in a rough game of Rock-Scissors-Paper. Alan was perched on the railing, his lower lip bulging with chew, his reddened eyes indicating that he'd already started drinking. Both Alan's parents were alcoholics, and apparently he was following right along in their footsteps.

"My mom wouldn't let me leave until I cleaned

up my room," Danica explained in a bitter tone. Wearing a frown, Danica's subtle attractiveness was replaced by the visage of an angry gnome with full cheeks, pug nose, and frizzy light brown hair that hung almost to her rear. At five one, she stood half a head shorter than the leaner, fairer-complected Jamie.

"And you should have seen it, looked like a war zone," Jamie added teasingly, taking note of the fact that Keith was looking at her rather strangely, as if he knew something she didn't. He was tall and lanky with shaggy brown hair and a boyish face, and on this late September morning he was wearing an oversized fuzzy blue sweater that made him look irresistibly cuddly.

"I've seen your room in worse condition," Danica countered.

Jamie shrugged. "My dad says I'm lazy, so I try not to disappoint him."

"So what are we gonna do about this place?" Alan piped up, then turned his head to eject a stream of brown spit. He was also tall but fairly thick around the middle, which was undoubtedly the result of all the liquor and beer he consumed on a daily basis. His parents hadn't yet noticed his pilfering or, if they had, didn't care enough to confront him. His hair was jet black, cheeks and upper lip darkened with manly stubble. His eyes, limpid pools of gray, appeared to be having trouble staying in focus.

"I say we kidnap the mayor's dog," Keith said, anxiously searching the faces of his friends for approval. Having met with only disparaging stares, he slumped against the slatted front wall of the depot. "It was just an idea."

Jamie flashed him a smile as she moved toward the depot's entrance, a pair of warped swinging doors lodged permanently inward. Each contained a dome-shaped leaded glass window which constituted the only areas not covered with graffiti. "Yeah, and a really dumb one, Keith. Try thinking of something we could say in a letter that would make him change his mind."

Stepping over the threshold onto heavily scuffed black and white linoleum, Jamie gazed nostalgically at the inner walls, also covered with familiar graffiti. Darren + Bobbi Jo = Luv 4-ever—1957. Long Live Elvis the Pelvis. Shayne Tidwell loves Rita Haines—1974. Let It Be. Motley Crue/Party on Dudes—SF'89. Jamie thought the graffiti alone made the old depot a very special place. A lot of sentiment had been scratched, painted, or penned on these walls, and though most of it was inane, it still displayed in its unique way the changing of generations, each marching to its own drummer. It was sort of like a museum. Maybe if the mayor could see it from that perspective, he'd leave it alone and find some other way to polish his image.

The others had followed her inside. Alan teetered over to one of the long wooden benches and dropped ungracefully onto it, making a sloshing sound that indicated he had a bottle or flask stashed somewhere on his person, probably in one of the pockets of his pea coat. Danica slowly wandered over to the abandoned oak ticket counter, looking everything over as if for the last time.

Keith came up behind Jamie and wrapped his arms around her, which made her jump slightly. "I got it," he said, bending down to rest his chin on her right shoulder. "We write the mayor an anonymous letter threatening to kidnap his dog. He brags about her being the best hunting dog in the county, so that oughta make him think twice."

Jamie was confused by Keith's sudden display of affection, but she didn't try to move away in fear of hurting his feelings. It wasn't as if they hadn't hugged before, but there had always been a good reason for doing it. Celebrating the stroke of midnight on New Year's Eve, for instance, or when one of them had a birthday.

"Keith, would you please forget about the mayor's prize hunting dog. Since when do would-be kidnappers send an advance letter of warning? All Shepherd would think after receiving a letter like that is how to go about keeping his dog safe."

Roman turned from writing *I found it and turned it over to the sheriff* under the anonymous inscription *I lost my virginity here.* "What about a hunger strike? Maybe we could get all the kids in town to go on a hunger strike until the mayor reneges. I know my mom would be on his back day and night. She goes nuts when she thinks I'm not eating right." Her concern was understandable; since early childhood Roman had looked as if he'd been scrounging meals out of garbage cans. His skin always had a sickly pallor, and he was hands-

15

down the scrawniest male senior at Deer Creek Heritage Academy, a fact that made him a frequent victim of the redneck jock squad. His eyes, large pale blue marbles sandwiched between thick white-blond lashes, peered out from behind gold wire-rimmed glasses that matched his flat top. "Well? Is that a great idea, or what?"

Alan belched. "Or what, I'd say. I, for one, am very fond of eating, and I refuse to starve on account of this heap. Let's all get drunk at my place and just forget about it."

"Not me," Jamie said resolutely. "I don't want this heap to go down." Keith still had his arms around her, and she was beginning to wonder if he was actually coming on to her. The idea was almost laughable, as long as they had been friends. She could vaguely remember the two of them building castles and tunnels in her sandbox and catching tadpoles down at the creek with his mother's tea strainer.

"I stand with Jamie," he said, choosing that moment to end the embrace and move a few paces away. Staring in the direction of the back wall where someone had painted a life-sized buck and doe posed peacefully at a stream, he crossed his arms over his chest. "Maybe this is a heap, but it's our heap. Where else are we or any of the other kids our age going to hang out? The stupid skating rink?"

"My place," Alan said, spitting tobacco juice on the floor. "Always got plenty of booze. And entertainment, too. None of you have ever seen my parents really get into it, have you?"

"Get real, Alan." Danica grimaced.

Having finished his witty contribution to posterity, Roman straightened up and thoughtfully tapped the end of his pen against his temple. Looking at him, Jamie found herself wondering where life's road would lead Deer Creek's little "Girly Man," as the jocks called him. Certainly he would not be returning here after graduating from Purdue, the prestigious university at which he'd been accepted. Whatever direction he took, he would probably go far, she decided. The underdogs often did, while their persecutors ended up eking out a mediocre existence. In the long run, beauty and brawn didn't matter very much. In the long run, it was brains that counted, and Roman certainly had plenty of those. Surely a stroke of genius was gestating beneath that scrub brush he called hair.

Just then a slow smile began spreading across Roman's face, the kind of smile that always accompanied a gem of an idea. Jamie smiled back at him. "Okay Roman, what's your idea?"

Roman's smile widened. "Drum roll, please."

"For crissakes, just spit it out," Alan grumbled, leaning over to spit more tobacco juice on the floor.

Danica glared at Alan. "What's your problem? Maybe his idea deserves a drum roll. Like yours deserved unanimous raspberries."

"Chill out, you two," Jamie sighed. "If we start arguing, we're never going to get anywhere." Turning back to Roman, she placed a hand on her hip and said, "Cut the suspense and just spit it out, Roman."

All eyes were on him. Roman let a few heartbeats of silence pass for added effect, then raised his arms in a gesture that said, "Here it is, a piece of cake, you simpletons," and opened his mouth to release one word.

"Suicide!"

The others' mouths fell open, but they were too stunned at first to say anything. Jamie could hardly believe what she'd heard. And she'd actually believed Roman had brains. He'd just proven that he had the intelligence of a weather vane.

Alan was first to speak. "Oh, now that's a brilliant idea, all right. I refuse to starve myself, but I have no problem at all with killing myself. So how should we do it? I've heard carbon monoxide poisoning is a nice way to go, you just fall asleep permanently, but that's not very dramatic. I say we should all climb to the top of the water tower and dive off."

"Roman! You are only joking, aren't you?" According to her anguished facial expression, Danica was more than simply surprised or shocked. Hugging herself and shivering as if suddenly cold, she stared at Roman with wide, pleading eyes.

"Of course he's joking," Keith said, but a look of uncertainty crossed his face. "Aren't you?"

Roman shook his head slightly and chuckled. "Come on, peeps, you know I'm not that stupid. I didn't mean that we should *do* it, just that we should *threaten* to do it. You know, send a letter like Jamie said, telling the mayor that if he continues with his plan to tear this place down, the five of us will kill ourselves. And we'll all sign it in our own blood, so it'll look like we really mean business. If that won't stop him, nothing will."

Jamie felt her smile returning as her faith in Roman's intelligence revived. He was absolutely right. His plan, though low-down and dirty, was their best shot. The mayor couldn't take the chance of having the citizens of Deer Creek think him indirectly responsible for their untimely deaths.

As far as she could see, there was only one drawback. There existed a strong possibility that word of the letter would get around and, in its journey through the small-town grapevine, reach her father's ears. Undoubtedly this would come under the heading of social embarrassment in his book, but was it her fault that he shared the same sense of humor allotted to drill sergeants and grizzly bears?

"I think that's a great idea, Roman. If my dad finds out, I'll probably lose my car keys for a month, but it'll be worth the sacrifice. Still, let's at least try to keep this a secret."

Keith nodded. "Sounds okay to me, except for the part about writing our names with our own blood. Can't we just dip our quills into a raw steak or something? I kinda doubt the mayor's going to send the letter off to a lab to have the blood analyzed."

Alan pulled a pint bottle of peppermint schnapps from one of his inner coat pockets and twisted off the cap. "Gotta hand it to you, Romano, you come off with a pretty good one now and then. Let's have a drink to celebrate." He closed his tobacco-stained lips around the mouth of the bottle and tipped it straight up, chugging several hearty swallows. Lowering the bottle, he then held it out to Jamie.

"No thanks," she said.

They all declined in turn. Alan shrugged, and proceeded to polish off the bottle himself.

"We need to get this done right away, before a ball starts rolling that not even the mayor can stop, like a signed contract," Jamie said, noticing uncomfortably that Keith was giving her that strange look again. "If we hurry, we can get it to the mayor's office before it closes at noon. I think I've got some notebook paper in my glove compartment."

"Good, now all we need is a raw steak. Anyone think to bring one along?" Danica quipped as she casually sauntered in Roman's direction with her hair pulled over one shoulder, hands jammed in the pockets of her jeans. For the first time Jamie noticed that Danica was starting to get a little pudgy around the middle. But that wasn't much of a surprise, considering her fondness for chocolate and sweets.

Jamie looked around at the others. Danica and Roman had retreated to a back corner where they were talking very quietly. They'd been doing a lot of that lately, and Jamie suspected there was something more intimate than friendship going on between the two, but for some reason neither of them would admit it.

"If everyone agrees, we'll spin Alan's bottle,"

Jamie said, her eyes flitting from face-to-face. "The one the neck points to gives the blood. That sound fair?"

After several seconds of meditative silence, everyone agreed, if somewhat reluctantly, that would be fair. They gathered in a circle in front of the ticket counter, generously spaced. Jamie had taken charge of the bottle, since Alan was having a hard enough time just standing up straight. Stepping forward, she crouched in the center and laid the bottle on its side.

"Well, here goes." She sent the bottle into a fast spin and quickly stepped back to her place, watching the revolutions as her friends were—with great trepidation. None of them were great lovers of pain.

"Please don't point at me," Roman implored aloud. "If my mom sees a cut on my finger, she'll probably rush me up to the hospital in Elk City for massive antibiotic infusions."

"We'll send a card," Keith grumbled.

Round and round the bottle went, slowing, slowing . . .

Danica stopped biting her lower lip long enough to say, "What is the unlucky winner supposed to cut him or herself with? A rock or a rusty tin can?"

"No way," Alan said with an adamant shake of his head. "I got my hunting knife up under the seat of my pickup, and I guarantee that baby is *shaaaarp*."

"Oh. I feel so much better now," Danica muttered sarcastically.

21

The bottle made its final revolution and pointed directly at Jamie. She groaned loudly. Danica, Roman, and Alan simultaneously sighed with relief, then Alan stumbled back to the nearest bench. Stretching out horizontally, he complained that he didn't feel so good.

Keith, suddenly a white knight, raised the spirit of dead chivalry, startling them all, except for Alan, who was too busy getting sick. "I'll do it for you, Jamie. It's no big deal to me."

Jamie squinted at him. This from the same boy who'd not so long ago laughed his butt off when she stumbled barefoot into a sticker patch? Who, when swimming in the creek, liked to drop live crawdads down the back of her bikini bottoms? Who'd teased her relentlessly for getting scared when they'd all gone to Elk City to see the movie *Candyman?*

"Thanks, Keith, but the bottle pointed to me fair and square. Besides, it's no big deal to me either." *What are you saying?* an inner voice squealed. *You hate the sight of blood, especially your own! And you've been known to cry over paper cuts!*

"What a woman." Danica smiled.

Roman paused in the midst of counting his lucky stars. "What an idiot, you mean."

Jamie silently agreed with Roman. "Well, I'll go get the paper out of my glove compartment. Alan, you—" She looked toward the bench and saw that Alan had passed out.

"—have a nice nap," she finished lamely, shaking her head and feeling very sorry for him. He came off as being the happy-go-lucky type, but he had to be totally miserable behind that facade, or he wouldn't drink so much. He joked constantly about his parents and their knock-down, drag-out fights, but down deep, those bitter, drunken feuds were surely tearing him apart.

"I'll get the knife while I'm at it," she sighed, and headed for the door. Behind her she heard Roman say to Danica, "Go with her to make sure she doesn't try to make a run for it."

"Very funny, Roman," Jamie called out without looking back.

She returned a few minutes later with a sheet of notebook paper and Alan's hunting knife still in its sheath. She was in no particular hurry to have a look at the *shaaa-arp* blade.

Roman, Danica, and Keith had seated themselves on the opposite end of the front-row bench where Alan was now snoring loudly.

Jamie handed the sheet of paper to Roman. "Here, it was your idea, so you compose the letter."

Silently Roman took the sheet of paper over to the scarred ticket counter and laid it down. After staring into space for several moments, he took the ballpoint pen from his shirt pocket and began to write. Jamie lowered herself on the bench between Keith and Danica.

"I wish you'd give me the knife."

Jamie glanced over at Keith, finding he had that weird moonstruck look in his eyes again. And for the first time in their long-standing relationship, Jamie looked back at him as a potential boyfriend instead of a regular friend, just to see how it would feel. She decided it felt very strange.

"I'm a big girl now, Keith. I can take it."

"For God's sake, let him do it," Danica said, nudging Jamie with her elbow. "What are you, some kind of masochist?"

Jamie's jaw set. "The bottle pointed to me, so I should do it. If it had pointed at you, I doubt if Roman would have offered to take your place."

"You doubt right," Roman muttered from across the rectangular, boxcar-sized room. His statement was punctuated by a hoglike snort from Alan.

"I'll remember that, Roman Alexander," Danica swore, her eyes narrowed into angry slits.

Definitely, there is something going on between those two, Jamie thought. But if they wanted it to remain a secret, far be it from her to blow the trumpet. Living in a small town was, to her, too much like living in a fish bowl as it was: privacy was a rare commodity. For sure she had faults, a few little ones, actually very tiny, itty-bitty minuscule ones, but having a long nose to stick into other people's business was not one of them.

"So what's with you, anyway?" Danica asked, bending forward to address Keith with an arched eyebrow. "Would you have offered to step in for me too, or have you finally been smitten by the love bug?"

Jamie gasped. "Danica! Get real."

Roman stopped writing and smiled in their direction. "First comes love, then comes marriage—"

Danica suddenly burst into tears.

Lips tightly compressed, Roman quickly turned back to the letter.

Jamie didn't know what to do or to think, but she had the sensation of being in over her head. Way over. An ugly suspicion arose. She pushed it back down. It rose again. Again she pushed it down. Danica was in some kind of physical pain, she firmly decided. Maybe her appendix had just ruptured or something. She placed her hand on Danica's shoulder.

"Are you in pain? Do you need to get to a doctor or hospital?"

Still sobbing, Danica adamantly shook her head.

Jamie looked to Keith. He shrugged, his expression clearly indicating that he didn't want to be dragged into it, whatever it was.

"Okay everybody, listen up," Roman announced briskly as he turned from the counter with the sheet of paper in his hands, acting as though nothing at all were amiss. "To whom it may concern. The old railroad depot may be an eyesore to some people, but to us it is a cherished resort, the only place where we can go and just be ourselves. It is also a nostalgic monument, its sentiments crafted by the hands of three generations. We will permit its destruction over our dead bodies. We mean this quite literally. We have made a pact, sealed by our own blood, that we will kill ourselves if the depot is destroyed. Signed . . ."

Roman looked up from the paper. "Well, how was that? Too sophisticated?"

Danica had stopped crying, but she still wouldn't

look up. Jamie had been so concerned about her friend—and ticked at Roman for being such an insensitive clod—that she'd hardly heard any of it. So she gazed back at him but said nothing.

"Sounded fine to me," Keith said, his voice sounding small in the overwhelming silence.

Alan mumbled something unintelligible, then farted explosively.

This broke them all up, even Danica, who immediately scooted as far from Alan as she could get without climbing into Jamie's lap. Their boisterous laughter awakened Alan, who groggily pushed himself into an upright position looking like he'd just gotten off the Tilt-O-Whirl at the county fair after a ten-hour ride.

"What's e'rybody laughing at?"

"Your speech," Roman answered almost straightfaced, then burst into another maniacal peal with Keith and the girls. By now Jamie was laughing so hard that tears were coursing down her cheeks. Seldom did she witness perfect justice, but this was definitely one of those rare occasions.

Alan was obviously having a hard time keeping his eyes focused. "What, was I talking in my sleep?"

"Loud and clear," Keith chuckled, and to demonstrate exactly what he meant, he pinched his nostrils together. Although Alan probably had the cognitive abilities of a rubber duck at the time, he got the picture, and his face blossomed red down to his collarbone.

"Quit laughin' or I'll do it again. Right in your

face!"

"In your dreams!" Keith shot back, but he did stop laughing, as did Jamie and Danica. Roman was obviously trying very hard to get it under control, but every few seconds a snicker escaped as he silently reread the letter he'd composed.

Jamie mused at how quickly and easily normalcy—if such a term could be applied to a group of teenagers—had been restored. All it had taken was a fart. Yet it wasn't the same as before. And she had the feeling it would never be the same again.

Still smirking, Roman lowered the letter and fixed his eyes on Jamie. "I think this'll work. All it needs now are our bloody autographs."

Jamie winced at the hunting knife in her lap. Too bad this couldn't wait until the next time she shaved her legs—then everyone in the county could write their names. Slowly, with trembling hands, she undid the snap and pulled the heavy blade from its leather sheath. It shiny surface gleamed menacingly, promising exquisite pain.

"You'd better be careful or you'll cut your whole finger off with that thing," Danica cautioned.

Jamie's face paled. "I can't do it. Somebody else has to do it for me. And whoever wants the job better hurry before I chicken out or faint. I feel a little of both coming on."

"Oh, give me the knife, I'll do it," Danica said, a little too enthusiastically, Jamie thought. She reluctantly handed the knife over, then stuck out the forefinger of her right hand and tightly squeezed her eyes shut, her lips pulled back in a grimace.

"Not too deep. I don't want you coming at me next with a regular sewing needle and thread."

Danica took hold of Jamie's extended finger, and Jamie tensed. Danica's hand was a little shaky too, she realized, which made her even more nervous. Terrible images flashed in her mind. Her mother taking one look at her and shrieking, "Jamie! Where is your right hand?!" But that was a bit extreme, hardly a real possibility. Hurry hurry hurry, she thought. However, lying on a hospital bed in the intensive-care unit receiving massive transfusions to replace the gallon of blood she'd lost from the cut on her finger, now *that* she could see. In full Technicolor detail.

"Come on, get it over with before I lose my nerve."

Danica surprised her by answering, "Relax, Jamie. It's already done."

Jamie could hardly believe it; she hadn't felt a thing. Gathering her courage, she opened her eyes to see how badly she was bleeding. But she wasn't. At all. What . . . ?

Looking up, she saw that Keith was now holding the knife, and there was blood dripping from a small cut on his left forefinger.

"I cheated," he said with a triumphant smile. Before she could get on his case about it he returned his gaze to the wound and called out commandingly, "So come on, people, let's do it. This isn't Old Faithful."

Jamie stared at him with mixed emotions. She

was a little angry that he didn't allow her to perform her rightful duty, but then she was also grateful he'd cared enough to do it for her. Maybe he was trying to make up for all those crawdads, laughing at her ooching and owwing in that sticker patch. Her mind refused to speculate further, but she suspected that later she would probably open up to her diary, as she usually did.

Roman had taken his ballpoint pen apart so they could use the open end of the ink dispenser as a quill. One by one, grim-faced and mute, they dipped the pseudo quill into the blood pooled around Keith's wound and signed their names. Jamie was last to sign, and as she watched her friends commit their names in blood to the paper, an inexplicable, eerie feeling stole over her, as if what they were doing was for real, as if they were actually signing their own death warrants. It caused a quiet shudder to run through her, and she had no doubt that some heavy-duty nightmares were forthcoming.

"Your turn, Jamie." Danica was offering her both the letter and the thin plastic cylinder, its hollow tip crimson with Keith's blood. Swallowing a sudden lump in her throat, Jamie took them from her and added her name to the list.

Chapter Two

Danica was unusually quiet during the ride to the mayor's office. And although Jamie was close to bursting with questions, she didn't allow any of them to leave her lips. But Danica didn't keep her in suspense.

"I'm pregnant," she blurted when Jamie obeyed the stop sign at the intersection of Main and Maple Avenue.

After what she'd witnessed at the depot this morning, the news didn't knock Jamie over, as it would have done the day before. But it was nonetheless distressing. Danica knew about birth control, so how could she have gotten herself into a mess like this? She might just have flushed her whole future right down the toilet.

"Roman's the father, I take it."

Danica nodded, her eyes lowered in shame. "He didn't want anybody to know about us, that we were going together, because he was afraid if his mother found out she'd have a stroke. I think the neurotic hag intends to keep him tied to her apron strings for the rest of his life. Anyway, for that same reason he refused to buy condoms. He was afraid that as soon as he left the pharmacy, Mr. Pinkerton would be on the phone to his mother. So we just used the rhythm method, otherwise known as Russian Roulette, but that was the only other option we had. You know what would've happened if I'd gone to get anything—the whole town would've found out."

"You don't think they'll notice your stomach pooching out like a basketball?" Jamie sighed, moving the Corsica slowly through the intersection. "Did it ever occur to you to use the knees-together method? That one's foolproof. So is complaining about a bad case of genital warts. But I guess it's too late now."

"Roman wants me to have an abortion in Elk City. He said he'd get me the money." Danica buried her face in her hands and started crying again. "I don't know what to do. He says he loves me, but with him college comes first. And I understand that, I know it's important. But so is a baby."

At that moment Jamie's feelings on the matter were admittedly selfish, glad that she wasn't in Danica's shoes, although several times in the past Jamie had offered to trade lives—and problems—with Danica when she complained of some petty little thing her parents or younger sister had done. You think you've got problems, Jamie would laugh cynically. Try having a dad who

31

thinks that unless you become a rocket scientist or first woman President of the United States, you'll be a complete failure.

If Keith happened to be around, he would then say to Jamie, "You think that's rough? How would you like it if your dad wanted you to spend the rest of your life shoveling cow crap when you wanted to be a rocket scientist? He told me if I deserted the family business to go to college so I could become some white-collared robot, he'd disown me."

Roman would pour out his grievances about his smothering, overprotective mother, which of course would make Keith's dilemma look trivial.

And lastly Alan would tell about all the times he'd seen a butcher knife go sailing across a room, and everyone else would be silenced. It was pretty hard to top knife-throwing. But that was before Danica got pregnant.

"I don't know what to tell you, Dan. I honestly don't." Jamie slowed the car; they were approaching the mayor's office, which was part of the same red brick building housing the Town Hall and its various offices, county courthouse, and the two-celled jail. A towering shade tree on the corner provided a leafy canopy over the cement steps leading up to the white double doors of the mayor's office. At this time of year most of the leaves were yellow and orange, and the ground was littered with those that had already fallen.

Just to the left of the double doors, set into the

wall at waist level, was a wide gold rectangle which was the hinged lid of the mail slot. Jamie pulled her car up to the opposite curb, put the transmission in park, and glanced at her watch. It was just a few minutes until noon.

"I hope nobody comes out while I'm doing this," she muttered under her breath. As she watched, a gust of wind gracefully swirled some fallen leaves on the sidewalk. A death dance, she thought grimly.

Danica, whose face was now hidden between her hands didn't respond. Shaking her head slightly, Jamie grabbed the folded piece of paper off the dashboard and stepped out into the street, where she looked both ways before dashing across. She had just slipped the letter into the slot when one of the white doors opened behind her.

She spun around wearing the guilty expression of a child caught with her hand in the cookie jar. And when she saw who'd stepped out, she felt all the blood in her body drain into her toes.

"Dad . . . uh, hi."

Hamilton Fox looked her over quizzically for a few moments, wilting her with his dark, penetrating eyes. Eyes that said, *We have ways of making you talk*. "What are you doing here, Jamie?"

What was she doing here? Oh yes, she was delivering a letter to the mayor that in essence declared that if he tore down the old depot, she and her friends would kill themselves. What else would she be doing at the mayor's office? So,

33

Dad, what's new with you?

"I was—I was—I was looking for you," she stammered, attempting to smile. An inner voice promptly asked how idiotic she could get (as if she hadn't just given a demonstration). Now *why* was she looking for him? Actually, that was an easy one. Why was she ever looking for him? "I need some money for . . . gas. My tank's almost on empty."

She was so sure, so positive that he was going to ask how she'd known to look for him here, which she absolutely could not have answered without hanging herself, that she could feel herself starting to sweat although she normally didn't perspire even when the weather was hot and muggy. But having presented him such a ripe opportunity to jump on his soapbox, she needn't have worried.

"Again, already? What have you been doing, taking trips to California? Money doesn't grow on trees, young lady, a fact which apparently has not yet sunk into that thick skull of yours. Don't expect me to be giving you gas money when you're thirty-seven. But undoubtedly you'll be asking anyway, since by then you'll know just how far a Dairy Queen employee's paycheck will go. Unless, of course, you get smart now and start thinking seriously about your future."

Hamilton Fox was an imposing man, tall and broad-shouldered with a solid, impervious look about him. His dark blonde hair, worn military

34

length, was beginning to recede above the temples, vaguely making him Jack Nicholson without the double chin. Yet despite his foreboding appearance, Jamie couldn't remember a single time that he had ever taken a hand to her or to her older brother Jefferson, who was now at OSU earning an electrical engineering degree. No, Hamilton Fox's punishment of choice was grounding, which had meant sitting in a corner when she and Jefferson were little. It wasn't much of a deterrent to a teenager who was more than happy to be left alone. Jamie felt rebellious words rising up within her, but fortunately her brain kicked in for once and reminded her that this was a very bad time to mouth off.

"I'm trying, Dad, really I am. So can I have twenty dollars? I'll clean out the garage." By this time next year, she added silently.

Hamilton Fox sighed and reached back for his wallet, as Jamie had known he would. But he seemed to be moving with deliberate slowness, and Jamie was all but jumping out of her skin thinking that the door was going to open again and the mayor would come out waving that letter like a flag. If she was lucky, she would be grounded for five to ten. Years. Glancing across the street, she saw Danica peering worriedly in their direction through the driver's-side window. When Jamie looked, Danica put a hand to her throat and pretended to choke herself, her eyes and tongue bulging convincingly. Jamie averted her gaze quickly before Danica could make her laugh. This was not a good time to laugh, either. Her father would probably want a full explanation, and seconds were precious.

Finally, at long long last, he placed cash in her palm. "Now, Jam—"

"Thanks, Dad!" Jamie jumped up and kissed him on the cheek, which she hadn't done in years, and quickly trotted down the steps, pausing only a second at the curb to look for oncoming traffic before dashing across the street. "Bye! See you later! Tell Mom I'll be home for supper!"

"I think I'm having a heart attack," she muttered softly as she slid behind the steering wheel. Pulling her door closed she smiled and waved briefly at her father, then turned the ignition key, revved the engine, and took off down the quiet, tree-lined street as though it were the Indy 500 raceway.

"What a close call," Danica mused, craning her neck to watch Jamie's father through the rear window. "I saw him come out and thought for sure you were busted. What did you tell him? Did he know you'd put something in the mail slot?"

Now that her father was just a tiny blur in the mirror, Jamie relaxed her grip on the steering wheel and settled back in her bucket seat. "If he'd come out a second earlier I think he would have caught me. I couldn't believe it when I saw him, but his being there really wasn't that weird. Dad personally handles the city's account, which he

36

calls the Mount Everest of financial headaches."

Danica abandoned her rear-window vigil to stare straight ahead. "Since they sorta know each other, you think the mayor will tell your dad?"

Jamie shrugged.

"Well, I hope this little scheme works, 'cause I imagine we're all gonna end up in hot water over it. So where are we going? Not my house, please. My mom'll find some other chore for me to do."

"Dad gave me twenty bucks." Jamie smiled, pulling the folded bill from her blue-and-gray-striped flannel shirt pocket. "How about lunch at the Ace Cafe? Then we can go to Woolworth's and buy ourselves some new earrings."

In stark contrast to her black mood earlier, Danica broke into song. Wearing a theatrical grimace, Jamie turned on the radio to drown her out.

In Deer Creek on a Saturday night, the public service message "It's ten o'clock — Do you know where your children are?" could be answered confidently by every parent of a teenager: "At the old depot." But that would soon be changing, according to the article in that Saturday morning's *Review*. The prospect of the building going down didn't really bother the adult sector, although eyebrows had raised over the amount of tax money Mayor Shepherd was wanting to spend on that memorial statue with all its trimmings to be erected in its stead.

But at least one man in Deer Creek had been elated to ecstatic proportions by the news, and that man was Morey Monroe's father, Malcolm, Shepherd's opponent in the upcoming mayoral election. Morey knew his father could see straight through the incumbent's actions to his self-serving motivation, but in his father's opinion, Shepherd was cutting his own throat. Even though the depot was an old run-down place, it meant a lot to the kids in the community.

"What'cha smiling about, Dad?" Morey asked.

Malcolm Monroe looked up from his dinner plate, startled. "I'm sorry, Morey. Did you ask me something?"

Fortunately for Morey, he'd taken after his mother in the looks department, inheriting with her finely crafted features her dark, creamy complexion and abundance of glossy jet-black hair. But in every other way he was his father's son. "I asked what you were smiling about. You were sitting there looking like the cat who'd just ate the canary."

"Who had just eaten," his mother corrected. "Or who just ate."

"He knows what I meant," Morey grumbled.

His father gave him a sly wink which told him to humor her for the sake of peace, so Morey grudgingly repeated his statement correctly.

Casually hooking an arm over the back of his chair, Malcolm gave his son another smile which was more the conniving, stalking the canary type. "I assume you're planning to congregate with your peers at the old depot tonight as usual."

Morey had just shoved another forkful of lasagna into his mouth. He shrugged, knowing better than to speak with his mouth full around his mother, who, besides being the Grammar Police, was also the Manners Police. After washing the bite down with a swig of iced tea, he answered somewhat meekly, "Well, I kinda thought I'd stay home tonight and fool around with my computer."

"You can do that anytime," Malcolm countered, his voice booming with authority. "I want you to go to the old depot and find out how your friends feel about Shepherd tearing it down. I'm presuming they're as outraged as you are. And, Son," he added in a lower, more conversational tone, "be sure to let them know they have Malcolm Monroe's sympathy."

It was almost eleven P.M. when Jamie heard a sharp tap on her bedroom window. She had just dozed off, lulled to sleep by the boring historical romance she'd been reading. She could have spent the evening watching television with her parents, but that would hardly have been a trip to Disneyland. She'd much rather have been at the depot, of course, but she'd been grounded for the rest of the weekend by her father for driving like "a reck-

39

less fool" that afternoon. A child could have darted into the street from between parked cars, he'd stormed, and she would have had no time to stop. Jamie had acknowledged this as truth, and feeling duly contrite had gone straight to her room after supper.

Her eyes fluttered open and she bolted upright when the sound was repeated. It sounded like someone outside was throwing pebbles or something at her window.

Tossing the paperback aside, she scrambled out of bed and rushed over to it. Pulling the rose-colored curtains aside, she peered down at the shadowed lawn below. Sure enough, there was a dark figure framed between two of the Colonial-style porch pillars supporting the eave. The porch light wasn't on, so she couldn't be certain, but she had a sneaking suspicion that it was Keith. The white knight come to rescue his maiden fair. The thought didn't make her smile. Instead she wished she hadn't come to the window, so he would've assumed she was asleep and gone away. Keith had been like a brother to her all these years; she couldn't bring herself to think of him in any other way.

But it was too late now. He had seen her silhouette in the lighted window, because now he was waving. Halfheartedly she waved back, then slowly lifted the window, careful not to make any noise.

Leaning over the sill, she hissed down at him,

"What are you doing here? Didn't Danica tell you I was grounded?"

He tiptoed up to the house so that he was directly beneath her. Craning his neck to look at her, he responded in a loud whisper, "I've gotta talk to you. Can't you step out for just a few minutes?"

She almost asked him why he just didn't call her on the phone, but she already knew the answer to that. Hormones were calling the shots today. Then she noticed that something was amiss, there was something wrong with his face, and the question of raging hormones was pushed to the back of her mind.

"Keith, have you been in a fight?"

"I thought you'd never notice. That's what I want to talk to you about."

"With who?"

He stamped a cowboy boot impatiently. "Come out here, will ya? I'm gonna get a sore neck trying to talk to you like this. Tell your folks you're taking out the garbage or something. I'll meet you around back." He promptly disappeared beneath the lower eave hanging over the garage, giving her no time to argue.

As she quietly closed the window, Jamie told herself there was no reason for her to get nervous. If Keith had gotten the crap knocked out of him tonight, he wasn't going to try anything weird, like kissing her. But what if the other guy looked a lot worse? Then maybe Keith was feeling his oats.

"Oh, Lord," she sighed, padding barefoot across the champagne-colored pile carpet to slip on her shoes. Why did a teenager's life always have to be so complicated? Sometimes she wished she could have stopped aging at four. Those were the days. No school, no worries, no pressure about the future. And her love life had been a solid and secure affair with a stuffed chimpanzee who almost never got out of line.

Negotiating the stairs slowly in semidarkness, she wondered who Keith had fought and how the fight had gotten started. Keith wasn't one to start fights, but if pushed, he would definitely push back, and hard. Her first guess was that Alan, drunk as usual, had mouthed off one too many times. He and Keith had gone a few rounds in the past. She just prayed it had nothing to do with Morey Monroe, whom she still had a secret crush on.

All of the downstairs rooms were dark, testifying that her parents had already gone to bed. This was good. Jamie knew that her father would have smelled a rat if she'd suddenly had an urge to take out the trash, especially this late on a Saturday night, when normally she had to be reminded a minimum of five times. Occasionally threats of bodily harm were required. Jamie knew they were idle, but at that point she never pushed her luck.

Feeling more than seeing her way through the

kitchen, she reached the utility room, closed the door behind her and flipped on the light switch. The harsh 100-watt glare temporarily blinded her, causing her to stumble over a pile of laundry getting to the back door. Uttering a mild curse under her breath, she pulled the door open. Keith was standing just on the other side of the storm door with his face mashed against the glass. Unprepared for the hideous sight, a shriek escaped Jamie's throat. Keith backed away laughing.

Silently seething, Jamie unlatched the lock and pushed through the glass door, joining him on the patio. "Very funny, meathead. Keep on laughing and you're going to have two black eyes."

He sobered at once. "Sorry, but you should have seen the look on your face."

In the light shining through the opened inner door of the utility room, Jamie was now able to see Keith's face clearly, and it didn't look much better than it had pressed up against the glass. Not only did he have a beaut of a swollen shiner, he had a fat lower lip and an ugly gash across his left jaw that was still oozing blood. Dried blood was smeared on his left cheek and shirt collar.

"You should see your face. Looks like you've gone ten rounds with the Tasmanian Devil."

Keith's expression suddenly clouded. "No, but you're close," he grumbled, examining the scraped knuckles of his right hand. "It was Tommy Davidson. Lisa Gayle had told everybody she'd broken up with him this afternoon, so when he

43

showed up at the depot I knew there was gonna be trouble, the way she was flirting with all the guys. Even Roman. I noticed Danica didn't seem to like that very much; she looked ready to pull Lisa Gayle's hair out by the roots. Anyway, Tommy made some unflattering remark to Lisa Gayle, and Roman told him to shut his face. Good ol' Rome was feeling no pain at the time, and the circuits leading from his usual good sense to his mouth were temporarily out of service. Well, Tommy—"

"Finish telling me inside," Jamie interrupted, shivering as a chilly gust of wind swirled around them. "I'm getting cold, and besides, you need to get cleaned up, you're a mess. Need to get an antiseptic on that cut, too. It's okay, my parents are already in bed. We have to be quiet, though."

"I'll be quiet as a mouse," Keith promised.

In the kitchen, the first thing he did was bump into the dining table, knocking over the brass candelabra centered on it. The heavy stand hit the oak surface with a loud *KERTHUNK!*

"Way to go, slick!" Jamie hissed over her shoulder. Frozen in place by dread, she listened for the creak of floorboards overhead indicating that one of her parents was getting up to investigate the noise. All she heard was her own shallow breathing and Keith's low grumblings over his new injury, which was totally her fault. He wasn't a freakin' bat with built-in radar. She should have left the utility light on so he could see where he

44

was going.

Making a face at him that he couldn't see, she guided him to the kitchen sink, then stepped over to switch on the mellow stove light. "You've only been over here five thousand times," she whispered harshly as she pulled out a narrow drawer in search of a clean dishrag. "You should know where the stupid dining-room table is by now."

"Don't you mean, 'You should know where the dining room table is by now, *stupid?*' " Keith leaned back against the counter and hooked his thumbs in the belt loops of his Levi's, striking his practiced Cool Dude pose. "Sorry, but my head got used for a basketball tonight. Boy, I hope you don't decide to become a nurse. You'd make a really lousy one."

"Don't worry," Jamie muttered as she wet the dishrag and daubed it with soap. "My dad's sure I'll end up working behind the counter at Dairy Queen. So go on with the story. What happened after Roman told Tommy to shut his face?"

Keith winced as she began gently dabbing at the cut on his jaw. "As you can probably guess, Tommy didn't like it very much. In fact I'd say he was all over Roman in about two seconds flat. Everything happened so fast that the rest of us kinda just stood there about ten seconds watching it go down with our jaws dropped to the floor, listening to Roman squeal under Tommy like a stuck pig. The next thing I knew, Danica was running up behind Tommy swinging her purse and she whacked him across the back of the head with it. She must have had a brick in it because Tommy went flying like he'd been hit by a truck. It was really radical. But unfortunately it didn't knock him unconscious." To emphasize just how unfortunate that really had been, he made a woebegone face that made Jamie think of a hurt puppy.

"Unfortunately for you, not Danica," Jamie guessed.

"You have guessed correctly," he responded in a voice mocking game-show hosts. "So you win the grand prize, a fun-filled date in the exotic golden city of Deer Creek, Oklahoma, with none other than the incredibly good-looking sex god Keith Maguire!"

Jamie cocked her head and gave him a quizzical look. "And how hard were *you* hit on the head, Mr. Sex God?"

Keith's face instantly fell into a wounded pout, his eyes again drooping in the hurt puppy-dog tradition. "You insult me, Madam."

"I'll do more than that if you don't hurry up and finish telling the story," Jamie retorted, glancing nervously in the direction of the kitchen doorway. "In case you've forgotten, this situation could get me in a lot of trouble."

To herself she had to admit that the real reason for getting him back on track was to squelch the outrageous subject of their going out on a real date together, just the two of them, supposing he hadn't been jerking her chain. Considering his odd behavior at the depot earlier today, she didn't think he was. But she wished he was. She loved him, yes, with all her heart, but only as a friend. She didn't want to hurt him. Suddenly she felt a deep twinge of guilt, remembering that she'd forgotten to thank him for cutting himself in her stead. That must have hurt.

"Not really much left to tell," he said with a shrug, and Jamie could see that he was no longer trying to be cute. He'd seen the writing on the wall; she didn't have to draw him a picture too. She searched his face for any sign of emotional pain, finding only total weariness. "Tommy got up and started toward Danica. You should've seen the look in his eyes. Pure murder. And he said it, too, he said, 'I'm gonna kill you for that, you bitch.' I was afraid he was really going to do it, so I stepped in front of him before he could get to her and told her to run. Then I saw Tommy's right fist making a trajectory toward my face. I meant to duck, but I wasn't quite fast enough. His class ring is what made the gash. Anyway, to make a long story short we did the King Kong-Godzilla waltz for a while, him leading, of course. Then Alan jumped into it like Rambo on steroids and bopped Tommy a good one with an empty bottle—broke his nose, I think. While Tommy was keeled over howling about that, everybody scattered."

Eyes cast downward, Jamie shook her head in

wonder. "Wow, sounds like I really missed a good show."

"Yeah, too bad Morey Monroe didn't have his dad's camcorder with him. We could've made copies and sold 'em. Big bucks."

At the mention of Morey's name, Jamie felt a queer fluttering in her stomach "Morey was there?"

"Yeah, doing PR work for his old man, seemed like," Keith answered, his eyes boring intently into Jamie's when she looked up at him. "Why? You have the hots for him or something?" Jamie could see the pulse throbbing on Keith's neck, and the rhythm had suddenly speeded up.

He was scared. Oh God, poor Keith. He felt so bad already; she just couldn't say yes. She'd never once lied to him before, but if ever there was a time to start, this was it. "Morey Monroe, are you kidding? Of course not. He's too much of a pretty boy, and I've heard he's stuck on himself."

"He's good-looking and rich. Goes with the territory." Keith glanced at the clock on the oven. "Well, guess I'd better head for the farm. Gotta get up at early-thirty to take up my trusty shovel."

"Thanks for coming by to tell me what happened," Jamie said lamely, biting her lower lip. "And also for, uh, supplying the 'ink' for me today." She wanted to give him a kiss on the cheek to both thank him and offer silent apology for not feeling the same way he did, but she was afraid he would take it the wrong way. "When you get home, get some antiseptic on that cut so it won't get infec—"

Directly behind her, a deep voice suddenly boomed, "Jamie Lynn! What the devil's going on here?"

Jamie jumped a good six inches off the floor. Keith simply paled.

Heart thrashing in her chest, Jamie reluctantly turned to face her father, who was standing imperiously in the kitchen doorway in his pajamas and robe with his fists on his hips, a look on his face that could scare the hide off a buffalo.

I'm grounded for life, she thought.

But he wasn't quite that angry. After Keith left, she was sentenced to two weeks starting on Monday.

All day Sunday, starting at noon, when she finally got out of bed, Jamie was as nervous as a cat in the dog pound, nearly coming unglued every time her parents' line rang. She just knew the mayor was going to call her dad about the suicide pact, and then she really would be grounded for life, that right on top of last night's incident.

Danica called around three with a slightly altered rendition of last night's fight at the depot. According to her, Roman had been sweeping the floor with Tommy, but then Tommy had grabbed one of Alan's empty liquor bottles, obviously intending to use it as a weapon. That's why she'd hit Tommy on the back of the head with her purse (which did not have a brick in it. Just a "few" items of makeup).

She then went on to tell Jamie how sick she'd been all morning *and* afternoon. She'd thrown up three times, remaining constantly nauseated. Her parents were getting suspicious, she could tell.

"Oh God, Jamie, what am I going to do? I can't stand this anymore. Every time I smell anything at all I get sick, and you wouldn't believe how acute my sense of smell has gotten. I can smell the Claybornes' henhouse from my bedroom. What's even worse, I can smell my feet."

Jamie couldn't help but snicker. "Try washing them, dummy."

"I did, but they still stink. Everything stinks. By the way, are you wearing Obsession?"

Jamie was, but she didn't for a second believe Danica could smell it through the phone. "Listen to me, girl. I think it's time you fessed up to your parents about this. You sure can't hide it from them forever . . . unless maybe you decide to do what Roman suggested."

There was a long span of silence, then, "I couldn't live with that on my conscience."

"Then, you should go to your parents, let them help you to decide on another alternative."

"You mean putting the baby up for adoption," Danica responded curtly.

Jamie sighed. One thing she would never, ever

be, whether hell froze over or not, was a guidance counselor. "Did I say adoption? No, I said another alternative, and adoption is certainly one, but not the only. Maybe your parents would agree to raise your baby while you finished school and got yourself established."

Brash laughter assaulted Jamie's ear. "Oh yeah, I can just see my parents going for a deal like that. Like my mom hasn't seen enough diapers. She'd spin right through the roof. You know as well as I do they'd agree with Roman."

Jamie was fast becoming exasperated. What was Danica expecting her to do, wave a wand and make all her problems magically disappear? Encourage her to run away? Jamie hadn't caused the problem. She didn't see why she should be responsible for coming up with a solution.

"You should have thought about all this before, Danica."

"Like that really helps me now," Danica shot back angrily, but Jamie could detect the tears in her voice. "Thanks a lot for nothing, *friend!*"

There was then a click, and Jamie was listening to the dial tone.

Chapter Three

Jamie didn't wake up Monday morning in the greatest of moods. Just as she'd predicted, her sleep had been plagued by a series of nightmares. In the one she'd had just before waking, Mayor Shepherd was the Devil and somehow the letter they'd all signed with Keith's blood had turned into an agreement in which they agreed to pay for the depot's continued existence with their souls. Then only a few days later the depot completely crumbled with age, falling in on itself to make an indistinguishable pile of rubble. Unfortunately for them, there had been no soul-back guarantee.

Later that morning, when Jamie was reading the front page of the *Deer Creek Review* while her hot breakfast was being prepared, she came across a small notice that made her think that the nightmare might have been symbolically prophetic. Near the bottom of the page under the bold heading "Mayor Stays Course" she read, "In a statement issued from the mayor's office Sunday afternoon, Mayor Shepherd announced that in spite of the phone calls and crank letters he has received from local teenagers denouncing the demolishing of the old railroad depot, plans will proceed as scheduled. 'The building is hazardous,' the mayor says. 'It should have been torn down long ago. I can only hope that the kids opposed to this idea will come to understand that I truly have their well-being at heart. I'm not out to persecute them.' As previously stated, the operation will begin a week from today."

Next to the "Mayor Stays Course" article was a story about Letitia Gilbert, an elderly widow who lived next door to the Presbyterian church with about two hundred cats. Seemed that one of them, spying what probably looked like a nice cozy place to nap, had slipped into the clothes dryer when she wasn't looking. When Letitia had found her static-free, tumble-dried — and stone dead — cat, she'd suffered a heart attack, but it was a minor one and she was expected to recover.

Jamie was sorry for the cat, glad for Letitia, and absolutely furious at the mayor. Crank letters! How could he possibly know they hadn't been deadly serious? Where did he think that blood had come from, road kill? How dare he call their bluff!

"Jerk," she muttered under her breath.

Her mother turned from the stove. "What was that, dear?"

Jamie angrily shoved the paper to the other

side of the table. "Oh, nothing. I'm just not in a very good mood today."

The sky that morning matched her mood, a gloomy umbrella of massive gray clouds that hid the sun completely. As she drove to school, taking her time, Jamie wondered if Danica was still mad at her, if she would act as if nothing had happened or give her the cold shoulder. This wasn't their first spat, but all the previous ones had been pretty trivial and they'd always made up the next day. Jamie really didn't think she'd done anything wrong, but obviously Danica felt totally let down. So there was no predicting how things were going to be today, especially when she considered the fact that Danica's pregnancy probably had her emotions in a blender. Jamie remembered her mother telling about the time she was pregnant with Jefferson and cried for hours because her favorite soap-opera character had been wrongfully accused of stealing some jewelry.

But her speculating had been in vain; it was clear by the time the second bell rang that Danica hadn't come to school this morning. Her desk remained clear, and for some reason that empty chair seemed slightly ominous to Jamie, although she was sure Danica was only suffering from morning sickness. Roman was bent over his desk directly in front of Danica's, doodling absently on his notebook cover. Keith and Alan (and

Tommy Davidson) were in the other senior class. There were only two, and the three teachers who taught all the twelfth-grade-level subjects did the rotating.

In Jamie's room, first period this semester was American Literature taught by the infamous small-minded spinster Regina Frupp, otherwise known as Miss Brown Buns of Deer Creek.

"All right, class," Miss Frupp began with her prim little smile, clasping her hands together. "Who can tell me something about the Puritans? What were they like?"

Jamie almost piped up and said, "Just like you," then thought better of it. She was in enough trouble already. Her mind drifted from the subject being discussed to the long row of open windows across the room. The sky had darkened even more, promising a doozy of a storm. Jamie silently prayed it would knock out the city's power so they could all go home. Low thunder rumbled in the distance, sounding like a bowling ball rolling down a bumpy lane.

A few seconds later she found herself staring dreamily at Morey Monroe, who sat on the front row closest to the windows. The guy was such a hunk and there were always at least half a dozen girls clustered around him before and after school and in the cafeteria during lunch break. Needless to say, because of this he wasn't very popular with some of the other guys, but Morey was never picked on. He wasn't that big, but he had an air about him that warned it wouldn't be a good idea, like maybe he had a black belt in karate that he felt no need to brag about.

He caught her staring at him before she had time to avert her eyes and feign interest in something else. Now paralyzed by his returned gaze like a deer entranced by headlights, all she could do was blush and smile. To her surprise, he winked and smiled back, and that broke the spell. Jamie quickly turned her attention back to the front of the classroom, acutely aware of her racing pulse.

Miss Frupp was glaring at her. "What can you tell us about the Puritans, Jamie?"

Jamie slunk lower in her chair, grimacing. "They were pure?"

As usual, bedlam ruled during lunch break in the cafeteria, and as usual the stuff they were trying to pass off as food looked and smelled like it had already been eaten and regurgitated. Jamie decided to go with the vending machine, and bought herself a Snickers bar and a bag of Fritos. No one could say she was careless about nutrition.

Also as usual she shared the same table with Keith, Roman, and Alan. Danica's absence had a presence of its own.

"Danica sick today?" Alan asked Jamie as he scooted his chair closer to the table, the action causing a loud scraping noise that made all of them wince.

Jamie shrugged. "I don't know, I guess. She wasn't feeling too well Sunday afternoon." She tossed a glance at Roman, but he was struggling to open his milk carton, apparently oblivious to all else.

"I assume everybody saw Shepherd's little tidbit in this morning's paper." Keith jabbed a fork at the majorly gross vegetable medley on his tray and scowled. "I've got a sore finger for nothing, man. Shoulda known he wouldn't fall for something like that, it was way too radical."

Alan, seated directly across the rectangular Formica-topped table from Jamie, was looking longingly at her Snickers as she unwrapped it. "Hey, Jamie, gimme half your candy bar. I'll let'cha have a few swallows of my apricot brandy."

"In your ear, Alan," she grumbled, thinking about what Keith had said. The issue of the depot's destruction had been on a back burner since Morey had smiled and winked at her, but now that she was reminded of it, her bad mood returned like a vengeful headache. Turning to Roman she said, "So what do we do now?"

"Kill ourselves, just like we told him," Alan pouted, picking at the mystery meat before him. "Let all go jump off the water tower. I bet it would make Shepherd feel real bad for at least half an hour."

Knowing he was only kidding, no one bothered

to respond to his ludicrous suggestion. In response to Jamie's question about what they should do now, Roman shrugged and replied tiredly, "I said if that didn't work, nothing would. That's the ball game, if you ask me. He wins, we lose. No big surprise."

For a while no one said anything else. Outside, the heavens still rumbled with occasional thunder, but as yet there had been no rain. Jamie's eyes wandered about the large room with its pale green plaster walls, the sort you'd expect to see in a mental institution. Most of the acoustic ceiling squares were stained as the result of food-flipping contests, and the green-and-white-checked linoleum floor was highly polished but still bore at least a million black scuff marks. But at the moment Jamie was completely unconscious of all these things. Her attention was centered on a table near the exit doors, from which Morey Monroe was getting up with a disgusted look on his face. His gaggle of admirers tittered like chipmunks when he announced clearly above the din, "To hell with this slop, I'm going to Dairy Queen for some real food."

Deer Creek Heritage Academy had a closed campus, so this was a serious breach of regulation. No one was supposed to leave the grounds during school hours unless a parent had come to pick them up, or they had a verified medical excuse. Jamie admired Morey for having the backbone to buck the system so flagrantly.

"Don't let your eyes fall out of your head," Keith said sourly.

Jamie cringed inwardly, realizing he'd caught her staring at Morey. She began to question the wisdom of telling Keith Saturday night that she had no romantic interest in young Mr. Hunk Monroe. Her brain began a desperate search for a diplomatic response, but Roman spared her the effort of finding one by changing the subject.

"I didn't see Tommy around before the bell rang this morning, and I don't see him anywhere now. I hate to be overly optimistic, but do you think maybe he died of his injuries?"

Keith turned to him and grunted. "Hope all you want, but I doubt it. He's not here today, though, so enjoy it while it lasts."

"By the way." Roman paused, looking slightly embarrassed. "Thanks for stepping in between him and Danica. It should have been me, but I was already pretty well pulverized."

Jamie compared Roman's face with Keith's. Pulverized? Roman hardly had a scratch, but Keith's black eye looked worse than it had Saturday night, the discoloration much more vivid, and his lip was still swollen. The cut Tommy's class ring had made was covered with a small Band-Aid.

"What about me, don't I get any thanks?" Alan complained through a mouthful of the school's imitation food. "I'm the one who broke the bastard's nose. I got in a couple of good kicks, too."

Keith gave him a dirty look. "Yeah, and one of those good kicks landed on *my* left shin. Wanna see the gigantic bruise it made?"

"Wanna see my tit that he pulled?" Alan shot back, a few bits of meat spraying from his mouth. "Looks like a cow udder now!"

Visualizing what Alan had just described, Jamie couldn't help but laugh. "What is this, a competition for the Purple Heart?"

The bantering went on until lunch period ended, situation normal. In their reverie, awareness of Danica's absence grew dim, but Jamie was reminded when she returned to her classroom with Roman and saw Danica's empty desk. She decided then that in spite of her obligation to go straight home from school, she would stop by Danica's first and see how she was doing. Show Danica that she *did* care, which was really all she could do.

Danica's parents owned a small corner grocery store in the heart of downtown Deer Creek. They'd had six children; Danica was next to the youngest. And when the youngest had turned thirteen, Danica's mother had gone back to helping her husband run the store. That left Danica and her younger sister home alone in the afternoons, since the last of the older four children had recently flown the nest.

Looking at the "nest," it was easy to understand why they had been in such a hurry to leave it. The Hookers' house was little more than a shack with three tiny bedrooms. One of them—Danica's—was an add-on, which was very obvious from the outside since Danica's father had never bothered to cover the black sheathing. It sat along the southern outskirts of town with similarly dumpy residences, seedy trailer houses, and horse stables. The acre of land surrounding Danica's house was overgrown with a variety of weeds, and among the weeds lay discarded toys, old tires, car parts, and miscellaneous junk of every description. Some of it defied description. Jamie wouldn't be surprised if someone cleaned up the place and found Jimmy Hoffa.

As she walked up the gravel drive to the sagging front porch, the first drops of rain began to fall. Jamie remembered how much Danica always complained when it was rainy because her hair frizzed up even worse than usual. Once she'd tried to iron it, but she had the setting up too high and didn't protect her hair with a towel, so she'd come up with an iron-shaped empty space. By the time she'd finished cutting the rest of her hair to make it all even, she looked like Cleopatra.

Jamie had just stepped up to the front door when it began pouring, the rain jetting down forcefully in wind-driven sheets. Jamie wasn't a great lover of rain herself, but she was grateful for it today. It provided a very plausible excuse for her coming home late from school.

From the other side of the door, she could hear sounds coming from the television, a familiar commercial jingle. She knocked, three sharp raps, then thought about just walking in, like she usually did unless Danica's parents were home. But thinking of the way their last conversation had ended, she decided to wait.

A minute or so passed, and no one came to the door. Jamie wondered if Danica had peeked out one of the front curtains, saw her, and decided not to answer. She knocked again, this time a little louder. Still there was no answer, and no sound from within but the television.

Jamie considered leaving under the conviction that she was being purposely ignored, but instead decided to try the doorknob. Maybe Danica was in her bedroom plugged into her Walkman, or taking a shower and couldn't hear the knocking.

The knob twisted in her hand. Unlocked. Jamie slowly pressed the door inward, peeking through the widening crack. "Danica?"

No response.

"Darlene?"

Still nothing. But they had to be here; they wouldn't have run off and left the door unlocked, though Jamie doubted a burglar would have much interest in their place. But actually the inside of the ramshackle house was pretty decent, surprisingly so considering its surroundings. All the furniture was old and covered with patches and the carpet was threadbare in spots, but the place was obviously very clean, not a trace of dust in sight.

Pushing down an irrational fear that something was wrong, Jamie stepped inside and quietly closed the door behind her. The din of rain pounding on the roof was fairly loud, but after listening carefully for several seconds, Jamie determined that the shower wasn't running.

This time she shouted. *"Danica!"*

There was an old western movie on, the present scene involving a lot of whooping, hooting, and shooting that was making Jamie nervous. She turned off the set and started toward the back to the house, where Danica and Darlene's bedrooms were located. Passing through the kitchen, she noticed this morning's *Review* opened to the front page on the dining table.

"Danica?" Jamie approached Danica's bedroom door, which was slightly ajar and located at the end of a short, narrow hallway with dark-paneled walls and a dingy linoleum floor that creaked under her footsteps.

At the end of the hallway Jamie stopped, taking note of the fact that her palms were sweaty, her heart was thumping unusually fast, and there was a queasy feeling in the pit of her stomach. All symptoms of fear. She told herself firmly that there was no reason for her to be afraid. Danica was behind that door with speaker plugs in her ears, listening to Bon Jovi or Damn Yankees

63

while she doodled her and Roman's initials inside hearts and all that silly garbage or she wasn't here at all. Danica had too much on her mind to worry about whether or not she'd locked the door.

Pasting a smile on her face, Jamie pushed Danica's bedroom door open.

For a moment the sight that greeted her was too horrible to be believed. The smile she'd pasted on wilted instantly, but the rest of her body remained frozen in place. Then the truth slammed home, and Jamie fell back into the hallway, releasing a bloodcurdling scream.

Chapter Four

Sheriff Hank Hammond was short, fat, and ugly, bald as a balloon, yet the man had been married six times, a mystery that none could fathom. He wasn't much of a sheriff, either, with a reputation for chewing the fat even more than he chewed on chili dogs and pizzas. But then, the biggest crime in Deer Creek so far this year had been the sheriff's own house getting toilet-papered. The perpetrator of this heinous act was still at large, but no one, except maybe Hank, was losing any sleep over it.

Jamie was a little surprised to see his blue and white patrol car pull into the Hookers' driveway only five minutes or so after she'd made the call, but her mind didn't dwell on the marvel for very long. For the most part her brain was numb, still in shock from what she'd seen in Danica's bedroom. In the last five minutes she'd repeatedly told herself that it had just been some terrible hallucination. But it hadn't been. Down deep, far below the comfort of denial, reality had already sunk black fangs into her heart. Danica was dead.

She rose stiffly from the sofa and forced her wooden legs to carry her toward the front door. Through the gauzy yellowed curtains covering the front window, she caught a glimpse of someone with Sheriff Hank, probably one of his equally worthless deputies.

Opening the door, she glanced briefly at the sheriff's grave expression and stepped back with her eyes lowered. The lawmen entered, Hank placing a beefy hand on Jamie's shoulder as he passed. The small gesture of consolation instantly broke the dam holding back Jamie's reservoir of emotions. Shoulders hunched, she burst into wracking sobs, covering her face with her hands.

"There, there," Deputy Pete Dudley crooned, guiding her to the sofa while Hank continued tentatively toward the back of the house. Pete reached into one of his back pockets for a hanky and offered it to her, but Jamie shook her head, seeing through the haze of tears that it had already been used several times. She used her sweater instead, not caring in the least that she was getting mascara all over it.

"You just stay right here now and try to calm down," Pete said, then quietly left her to follow Hank.

They returned to the living room a few minutes later, Hank's normally rosy cheeks ashen. Pete, as skinny as Hank was fat, looked like he'd just gone for a ride inside a tornado. Nothing like this had ever happened in Deer Creek before.

"Dang it to hell, this is about that suicide note you knuckleheads sent to the mayor, ain't it?" Hank accused with his hands on his bulging hips. His earlier compassion for Jamie had completely evaporated.

His knowledge of the letter surprised her enough to stanch the flow of tears. "How did you know about that? Did the mayor tell you?"

"No, Louella over at the cafe did, yesterday mornin' when I stopped in for a cup of coffee. She heard it from Sally Tucker, who heard it from her son David. Don't know how David latched onto the news, but that ain't what I'm worried about. You done told me it was true, so what I'm worried about right now is what the rest of you knuckleheads are gonna do. Same thing as your friend in there?" He jerked a thumb toward the back of the house.

Shaking her head slowly from side to side, Jamie stood up. "No, and that's not why Danica . . . Sheriff, that letter we put in the mayor's mail slot has nothing to do with this. We weren't serious about it at all, it was just a bluff, a wild-hair idea we came up with to try and stop Mayor Shepherd from tearing down the old depot. None of us intended to carry out the threat."

"Looks to me like one of you was serious," he argued. Turning to Pete, he said in a surly tone, "Get on the phone and call Mr. and Mrs. Hooker at the grocery. Just tell 'em to come home, don't tell 'em what for till they get here. Then call

Smiley down at the funeral home and tell him he's got a customer."

His last words made Jamie start crying again. She couldn't believe the sheriff's callous attitude. He was acting as if Danica had committed a crime. Well, technically she had, but she still deserved respect. What she'd done was going to hurt other people, the people who cared about her, but her death was no less a tragedy, and Danica was no less a victim.

And she had most definitely *not* hung herself from her light fixture to honor that stupid blood pact, but Jamie had no intention of telling Sheriff Know It All the real reason. Jamie hoped the secret of Danica's pregnancy would be forever buried with her.

Finally she managed to say, "Did you . . . did you take her down?"

Hank nodded. "Yep. Laid 'er out on the bed."

His tone was such that he might have been talking about a deerskin rug. Suddenly Jamie had to get out of the house; it seemed to be closing in on her. She didn't want to be here when Danica's parents arrived, and Darlene, Danica's younger sister, could show up any second. Jamie was overwhelmed by her own grief. Seeing theirs would just be too much.

"Is it okay if I go now?" she asked Hank, who had sauntered over to the front window. The rain had eased considerably, but her question was punctuated by a booming crack of thunder that rattled her bones.

He turned, eyeing her with disdain. "I reckon. If I need you, I figger I can find you."

Sniffling, choking back her sobs, Jamie hurried out the front door and leapt from the porch to the weedy yard. She stopped halfway to her car and stood for several moments with her face lifted to the sky, welcoming the warm raindrops on her face. No doubt the sheriff was watching her through the window, calling her a knucklehead for standing out in the rain, but Jamie didn't care. Maybe she was a knucklehead. So what? At the moment, she didn't care about anything. Danica was dead.

She'd intended to go on home, but two blocks from her house she changed her mind and went to Roman's instead. So she might get grounded another two weeks. Big whoopie. Make it four, Dad, make it eight. It doesn't matter, because you can't make Danica alive again.

Mrs. Alexander answered Jamie's knock. Roman's mother was a book that definitely could be read by its cover. Her face was a map of worry lines, and she exuded a constant cloud of anxiety. She was painfully thin, and like her husband, ridiculously old-fashioned. Jamie had always thought of Roman's parents as the Ward and June Cleaver of Deer Creek.

Unable to pull up a smile, Jamie said solemnly, "I need to see Roman." She knew he was there, because Alan's pickup was parked out front.

"They're down in the basement playing pool," Mrs. Alexander responded in her gratingly shrill voice as she pushed open the screen door, permitting Jamie to enter. When she did, Mrs. Alexander took a good look at her and exclaimed, "Why, Jamie Fox, you're completely soaked! Don't tell me you've been out walking around in the rain? Don't you know you'll catch your death of pneumonia?"

Jamie dutifully wiped her wet shoes on the foyer rug, assuming that Roman's mother was actually more concerned about muddy footprints on her carpet than in whether or not someone else's child came down with pneumonia. "Is it all right if I just go on down, then?"

"Wait just a minute, Jamie, let me get you a towel so you can at least dry your hair. If you like, we can put those wet clothes in the dryer. I've got a nice terrycloth robe you can wear until they're done."

Jamie forced up a tiny smile. "I'm fine, really."

"Nonsense. Let me get you that towel," Mrs. Alexander countered, and turned to prance down the hallway leading to the linen cabinets, returning a few seconds later with a large fluffy pink bath towel which she proceeded to drape over Jamie's head. After giving Jamie's head a firm and thorough rubbing with the towel, Mrs. Alexander instructed her to repeat the same action as often as necessary, then sent her on her way to the basement with a final admonition to make use of the space heater that was down there somewhere. Roman could probably find it.

The door to the basement was in the kitchen. It

was closed, but the heavy-metal music being played below still filtered through it. Jamie felt her chest tighten as she turned the knob and pulled the door open. The music came up full volume then, much louder than she was ever allowed to turn up her stereo at home—of course, it was a different story when both her parents were away—but in spite of the volume she could hear the clicking of pool balls mixed with Roman and Alan's laughter. Ignorance truly is bliss, she thought glumly as she headed down the concrete steps, closing the door behind her.

Alan noticed her first. He pointed his cue stick in her direction and guffawed. "Look who's here, it's the Sheik of Deer Creek."

Roman had been leaning over the table taking careful aim, but Alan had just shot his concentration. He looked up, his face breaking into a wide smile when he saw Jamie coming down the steps with the pink towel still draped over her head.

"Ah, Sahib! What brings you across the burning desert sands to my humble tent? And where's Danica? Out watering the camels?"

Jamie fought back another onslaught of tears by concentrating on her ragged breathing as she progressed to the basement floor. The tightening in her chest had worsened, making the task of filling her lungs seem impossible. "No jokes, guys. Something really bad's happened. Roman, could you please cut the music?"

She didn't bother to explain that it had been one of Danica's favorite songs and she just couldn't handle hearing it right now. But Roman turned off his CD player without complaint. Obviously the look on her face and the sound of her voice, not to mention what she'd said, had knocked all the nonsense out of him, and out of Alan as well, for once. They both looked at her with solemn expectation.

"It's Danica," she sighed. Her watery gaze fell to the floor, and for a long moment the three of them stood mute and motionless. Only the muffled rumble of distant thunder broke the heavy silence until Jamie could collect herself enough to continue, although she sensed that the guys had already guessed what she was going to say. "She's . . . dead."

Her grim announcement was followed by another silence, this one as dark and deep as the grave into which Danica's body would soon be placed. Jamie couldn't bring herself to look at Roman's face, at the shock and pain that was surely registered on it. Within Jamie a seedling of guilt began to grow, accusing her of not offering Danica enough moral support. If Jamie had been a better friend, Danica would probably still be alive.

Alan was first to break the crushing silence. "That sum-bitch. That dirty low-down stinking bastard."

Jamie snapped out of her self-condemning reverie and looked at him quizzically. "Who?"

"Who do you think?" Alan gripped his cue stick so fiercely that his knuckles turned white, but above them his face had darkened. "Tommy Davidson, who else? He said he was gonna kill her for hitting him in the head with her purse Saturday night, and he wasn't at school today, either. Two plus two equals four, right? I say we go find him before the sheriff can throw him in jail and bash his head in. Or has he already been arrested?"

Jamie pulled in a deep breath and released it slowly, shaking her head. "She wasn't murdered, Alan." Now Jamie forced herself to meet Roman's stricken gaze, noting that he looked like he'd just been kicked in the gut by a mule. As well he should, she thought, refusing to feel any worse than she already did by carrying an additional load of grief for Roman. "She killed herself. Hung herself from the light fixture in her bedroom."

Surprise and confusion was added to the pain in Roman's eyes, but he said nothing and after a brief moment dropped his gaze to the floor.

Alan scowled, and muttering something unintelligible under his breath, he dropped his cue stick onto the pool table, pulled up a leg of his jeans, and reached for the small silver flask tucked inside his right boot. Screwing off the lid, he lifted it to his waiting mouth and began chugging.

"Sheriff Hammond thinks she did it because of the letter we sent to the mayor," Jamie said in a tone tinged with anger as she pulled the towel from her head. Wearily she lowered herself onto a cedar chest pushed up against the open side of the cement stairway. "But we know better than that, don't we, Roman?"

Roman threw a fleeting glance in her direction but still said nothing.

"I wonder who blabbed about the phony blood pact we made," Jamie went on, this time directing her statement at Alan. "I don't suppose you shot the breeze with David Tucker anytime this weekend?"

Lowering the flask, Alan wiped his mouth on a flannel shirtsleeve, his expression blank as he searched the murky depths of his brain for a memory. When it finally came to light, his expression suddenly turned sheepish. "He was running the Mobil for his dad Saturday. I had to get some gas late Saturday afternoon, and he was bored so he talked me into hangin' out with him awhile. I think he just wanted to get looped. Anyway, we both did, 'course I was already that way to start with, and I guess I did accidentally say something about our deal. But he swore he wouldn't tell nobody else."

"He told his mother," Jamie said stonily. "Only takes one match to light a fire. But there's no way to stop it from spreading. So that's it, I'm history. Thanks for nothing, blabbermouth."

Then Jamie noticed that Roman's shoulders were shaking, and with his chin resting on his breastbone, it became clear that he was crying. His pool cue clattered to the floor. Jamie instantly felt another pang of guilt. The death of a close friend, the ultimate catastrophe, was hanging like a black shroud over their heads, and here she was worrying about the trouble she was going to be in over that stupid letter.

"I don't understand," Roman sobbed, turning to lie across the pool table with his face buried in his folded arms. "I thought we had it all worked out."

At that moment the kitchen door opened and Roman's mother appeared carrying a tray of cookies and three glasses of milk. Carefully descending the treacherous steps, she chattered like a magpie, oblivious to the dismal emotional atmosphere below. "I know how you kids like to snack after school, so here's some cookies I made this morning, Roman's favorite, oatmeal and raisin. His father prefers my peanut butter cookies, but my personal favorite is chocolate chip. They're not exactly what you'd call nutritious, but they're so good I usually end up eating the whole batch, which is why I don't make them very often or I'd get as big as an elephant!"

Reaching the basement floor, she beamed a proud smile around the room, but it died on her lips when she finally noticed the despondent expressions on all three of their faces. "Oh dear. Is something wrong? Roman . . . ?"

Jamie quickly rose to her feet, leaving the bath towel piled on the cedar chest. "I've got to get home. Thanks for the cookies, Mrs. Alexander, but I'm pretty late as it is." She glanced at Roman, but he had buried his face in his arms again. Behind him Alan stood slumped with both hands behind his back hiding his flask. Even in the relatively dim light of the basement, she could tell that Alan's eyes were red, but for once Jamie didn't think liquor was responsible. Their eyes met briefly, then Alan sniffled and looked away. Feeling tears of her own coming on, Jamie called out a hasty goodbye and hurried up the steps.

By the time the story about Danica's suicide was printed on the front page of the *Review*'s Tuesday morning edition, most of Deer Creek's residents had already heard the shocking news through the grapevine. Along with the account of what had happened in their Utopic little community, they had been fed Sheriff Hammond's explanation for the tragedy. But just in case anyone's ear had been left out, there it was in black and white for all to see, starting with the third paragraph under the heading LOCAL GIRL HANGS SELF:

When asked if Miss Hooker had left a suicide note, Sheriff Hammond frowned and shook his head. "No, not exactly, but she signed this paper a couple days back sayin' she would kill herself unless the mayor changed his mind about tearin' down the old depot. And it was plain to see he wasn't gonna change it, so she up an' went lookin' for some rope. There's four other knuckleheads signed that paper too, mind you, so don't be too surprised if this same thing happens again."

To your knowledge, was the mayor aware of this paper? "To my knowledge, yes he was, but don't go blamin' this on Gene, now. A mayor can't let a few fool teenagers tell him what to do. 'Sides, he probably didn't think they really meant it."

After finishing the article—in which Sheriff Hammond went on to assure the residents of Deer Creek that there had been absolutely no sign of foul play in the death of Danica Hooker— Jamie solemnly refolded the paper and wondered where she could hide it. Her father had heard about Danica's suicide but by some miracle had remained ignorant of the letter. She couldn't imagine him knowing and not saying a word about it. Of course it was only a matter of time, but she wanted to keep his wrath at bay as long as possible. She was already carrying a thousand-pound load around on her shoulders; all she needed was for her father to stick his foot out.

Moving like a zombie, she got up from the table and walked over to the kitchen cabinet where the trash was kept and stuffed the folded newspaper down on the bottom. It was only six A.M., but Jamie had been up most of the night, dreading sleep because of the nightmares it prom-ised. Every time she closed her eyes she saw Danica hanging from that light fixture, her face a mottled purple, eyes wide open and bulging, swollen grayish tongue sticking out, reminding Jamie of Danica mock-choking herself in the car on Saturday for a laugh. The few times Jamie had dozed off, her subconscious had initially changed everything back to normal, with all five of them messing around at the depot, acting like retards, thinking of new ways to crack each other up. Then Jamie would look over at Danica, and Danica's face would be a horrible purplish color, and what had been a heart pendant on a gold chain around her neck had turned into a tightly pulled noose. The last time, Danica's bulging eyes had simultaneously popped right out of their sockets, and she'd screeched, "Peek-a-boo!" Jamie had screamed, but all the others had laughed.

Trudging back up the stairs to her bedroom, she decided that she might as well get dressed even though there would be no school today; it had been canceled in due respect of Danica's funeral, to be held that afternoon at the Southern Baptist church to which her parents belonged. At least the paper hadn't said anything about Danica's being pregnant, Jamie thought with numb relief. That meant there hadn't been an autopsy. Jamie couldn't stand the thought of her friend being carved up, but in her opinion it sure made Sheriff Hammond look sloppy. Maybe Porky the Pig would lose his position in the upcoming election, like he deserved. Jamie didn't think anyone was running against him, but she liked the idea of him and Mayor Shepherd keeping each other company in the unemployment line. Jamie had no doubt whatsoever that Gene Shepherd would lose his seat now, because in spite of Hammond's request that the good people of Deer Creek refrain from blaming Danica's death on him, she knew enough of them would anyway.

The funeral was scheduled for two o'clock, but last night Jamie, Keith, Roman, and Alan had arranged by phone to meet at the church an hour beforehand to give Danica a private farewell. Jamie was still firmly grounded, but of course the funeral warranted a temporary reprieve, and her mother said nothing about her leaving so early or about the missing newspaper. In fact, since hearing of Danica's suicide, neither of Jamie's parents had said much of anything.

Hearing the soft tap of a horn, Jamie went out the front door still struggling into her buckskin jacket. Keith's old blue pickup was parked across the driveway, tailpipe rumbling loudly. Jamie couldn't help comparing it to the new sleek fire-engine-red Ferrari that Morey Monroe drove, always wearing a pair of dark sunglasses that made him look so unbelievably cool.

The name's Bond. James Bond. And you, Jamie Fox, are the woman I want.

Both arms in her jacket now, Jamie opened the passenger door to the pickup and climbed aboard. Keith offered her a meager smile.

"Get any sleep last night?"

Pulling the door closed, Jamie sighed. "A little, but it was full of nightmares. How about you?"

"Same." He put the transmission in drive and

eased down on the gas, propelling them forward with an obnoxious puttering noise.

The radio in Keith's truck was between repairs, forcing them to bear an uncomfortable silence that neither could seem to break. Jamie found herself remembering the last time she and Danica had been together, specifically when they were on their way to the mayor's office to deliver the letter. What was it Danica had said? A baby's important, too. Yes indeed. Hit it, Danica. *Rock-a-bye, baby, from the light fixture . . .*

Jamie shuddered, jerking herself out of the morbid daydream. "What?"

"I didn't say anything." Keith gave her an odd look. "You okay?"

Turning her head toward the side window, Jamie fought to keep her mind focused on the passing scenery. "I could use a few days of sleep, but other than that, I guess I'm sort of mediocre. I just can't—oh, never mind. It doesn't really matter now."

Keith made a right turn onto Franklin Avenue, then left at the stop sign at the bottom of the hill, which took them past the Hookers' grocery store. The plate glass windows were dark except for the security lights in the rear; it was closed today, and the black wreath hanging over the front door announced the reason why.

"What are you talking about?" Keith prodded gently.

Jamie shook her head. "Never mind. I really don't feel like talking right now."

* * *

They were the first to arrive. Upon entering the church, Keith took Jamie's hand and gave it a comforting squeeze. She automatically squeezed back and allowed his fingers to become entwined with hers, thinking nothing of the intimacy. This was definitely one of those occasions in which such actions were not subject to suspicion.

One of the church deacons, Fred Stewart, met them in the reception room. Jamie recognized him from all the newspaper photos she'd seen of him holding up prize-winning bass. He was small, stoop-shouldered, and gray-haired, a retired postal clerk who had nothing better to do than work on perfecting the science of fish-catching. Except for Sundays, of course, when it was his privilege and honor to pass the deep money buckets around. In spite of the outdated woolen suit he wore that all but swallowed him, he looked almost naked without his fishing cap, Jamie thought, glancing idly at his fuzzy pate from which his ears protruded like open car doors.

In low, grave tones Fred asked if they were there to see Danica, as if there might have been half a dozen other reasons they had for coming. A smart-aleck remark came to mind, but Jamie kept it to herself. Instead, she simply nodded.

Fred gestured toward a set of white double doors to their left which were propped open. Centered in the space between them, a podium stood holding a white register and fountain pen. "She's in the chapel. As you go in, the family would appreciate having your names signed on the register."

Jamie let Keith guide her toward the podium. She kept her eyes on the floor, not wanting to look up when Keith stopped before the register to sign. But while she waited for her turn, listening to the soft, melancholy organ music being piped into the chapel, she gained the strength to confront what she feared. Surrounded by dozens of pink carnations, the white casket was lifted on some sort of collapsible platform near the front of the church. Jamie noted with horror that the upper lid was opened.

"Oh God, Keith." She felt her knees go suddenly weak.

"What is it? Are you going to faint?"

Jamie thought that was a good possibility, but she'd have to step inside the chapel to sit down, and presently the last thing she wanted to do was go inside the chapel. She lowered her head, blocking her peripheral vision with her free hand. "The casket. It's opened."

Keith slid his arm around her. "Haven't you ever been to a funeral before? They always do that. Well, just about always. They wouldn't if the body wasn't . . . you know, presentable. I think it'll be good for you to see Danica fixed up. You don't want your last memory of her to be . . . how she looked when you found her."

Closing her eyes, Jamie took a couple of deep breaths, then slowly nodded. "I'm sure you're right. Just stay close in case I decide to faint."

After Jamie scribbled her name in the register below Keith's, they walked together down the strip of bright blue carpeting toward the front of the church. Multicolored light glowed through the tall stained-glass windows in the west wall, and normally Jamie would have remarked on the beauty. Today she barely noticed it.

As they approached the casket, Keith's arm tightened around her. Several moments of reverent silence passed, then Keith cleared his throat in prelude to speech. "Looks like she's just sleeping, doesn't it?"

Jamie had silently made the same observation, and with considerable relief. The still, pale form nestled in pink satin was a two-hundred-percent improvement over the mottled nightmare she'd seen hanging from the light fixture in Danica's bedroom. "Yes. Too bad she'll never wake up."

Keith didn't respond.

Jamie's gaze drifted from the slight smile that had been permanently applied to Danica's lips to the frilly white blouse she was wearing. Jamie had never seen it before, and it was of an old-fashioned style that Danica would have said she wouldn't be caught dead in. The collar was high, buttoning all the way up to her chin. If her family was that concerned about making Danica look pristine, they should have put her in a nun's habit. Then suddenly the reason for the high collar dawned on Jamie, and she groaned inwardly. The rope marks.

"Girl, I wish you could wake up so I could kick your butt. How could you do this to us? How could you do it to your baby, if it was so important? You killed him too, you know." Saying her wish aloud made her a little paranoid, as she remembered immediately afterward the old adage "Be careful what you ask, for in a moment of folly the gods may grant it." But if Danica awakened at this point, Jamie was certain her feet could get her to Tulsa within half an hour.

Keith drew her closer to him, patting her shoulder. "Don't be mad at her, Jamie. She didn't mean to hurt us."

Wiping her tears on Keith's cotton cowboy shirt, which smelled faintly of laundry soap and Chaps cologne, Jamie responded bitterly, "Well, being mad feels better than sad. Besides, what difference does it make to her? She—" Jamie abruptly fell silent, noticing something she hadn't seen before. Pushing away from Keith, she leaned toward the casket to get a better look, and although her hair practically stood on end at the idea of touching Danica's pale, spiritless body, she reached out and timidly pulled back the section of long frizzy hair that framed the right side of its face.

Now the mark could clearly be seen, behind the earlobe and just above the high collar's lacy hem. Makeup had been applied to the area, but she could make out the perimeters of a small purplish oval about the size of a nickel. Jerking her hand back lest it suddenly be seized by a dead girl who didn't like people messing with her hair, she asked Keith in a half whisper, "What the hell is that on her neck?"

After a few moments of careful deliberation, Keith looked down at her with the stoniest of somber expressions. When he spoke, his voice was pitched much lower than usual. "Jamie. Hasn't your mother had that little talk with you yet? The medical term for that thing on her neck is a hickey."

Jamie shot him a dirty look. "I know what a hickey is, and I bet I know a lot more about sex than my mom," she retorted, "but that is not a hickey on Danica's neck. She never had one before, and I distinctly remember her saying once how cheap they made a girl look, and that she'd knock the crap out of any guy who tried to put one on her."

Keith crossed his arms, his face a chunk of granite now. "What do you mean, you know more about sex than your mom?"

Jamie rolled her eyes. Saturday night she'd assumed he had gotten the hint, that she wanted to maintain the status quo in their relationship, but here he was questioning her like a jealous lover. She was tempted to start tossing out fictitious names, but this wasn't the time or place. "I read a lot of books, okay? Now what about this?" She pointed at the darkened spot on Danica's neck. "And don't try and tell me the rope did this. There's no way."

Sensing that someone else had entered the

chapel, she turned to see Roman standing halfway down the aisle with his hands shoved deep in the pants pockets of his formal brown suit. She noted with mild surprise that he was even wearing a tie. "Roman," she called out softly, motioning with a wave for him to join them.

Keith moved to block Roman from her view. "Jamie, what's the big deal, what are you thinking?" he whispered in an agitated tone. "Roman's really hurting; don't upset him any more, nerfbrain."

Jamie heard his disparaging words and, just as she did with most of her father's equally vain utterances, promptly wiped them off her memory slate. Stepping around him, she met Roman at the head of the aisle and gave him a sisterly hug, then led him slowly up to the casket, ignoring the warning look she was getting from Keith.

Roman's breath hitched as his eyes, shiny with tears, lifted to view the body. "Oh God, Danica." The last syllable stretched into a low groan.

"Roman, see that small bruise on the upper side of her neck? Do you know how that got there?" Jamie wasn't really sure what she was thinking, but she had a very strong feeling that the simple puzzle pieces they'd put together no longer matched grooves; their rational picture of this unthinkable occurrence had suddenly become warped. Although not yet consciously acknowledged, there were two words floating just beneath the surface of Jamie's subconscious mind: thumb print.

Swallowing hard, Roman tentatively leaned forward, lips arched downward in a slight grimace. When he saw what Jamie was talking about, his eyes widened behind their gold frames. "Looks like a hickey, but I sure didn't do it. Danica told me she'd brand my face with a waffle iron if I ever did."

Jamie tossed Keith a brief smile of triumph before asking her next question. "When's the last time you saw her?"

With a heavy sigh, Roman hung his head. "Sunday night. We both snuck out and met at the depot at midnight. Talked until almost two in the morning." After a long pause dominated by the soft organ music, a sob escaped his throat. "She told me she was going to wait a few months, then go stay with her sister in Ponca City until after the baby was born. She'd decided to put it up for adoption. And I promised to marry her as soon as I got my bachelor degree. I meant it, and I know she believed me. Maybe that's why she killed herself? Nothing else makes any sense."

Upon hearing this, the notion that the small bruise was possibly a thumb print finally emerged from the darkness of Jamie's subconscious. In response, her heart began to drum fiercely against her ribcage, its galloping contractions spurred by an overload of adrenaline. A sense of dread enveloped her like a dense, cold fog. "Try this on for size. Maybe Danica didn't kill herself. Maybe her death was made to *look* like a suicide. I was thinking that the little bruise on her neck could have been caused by a thumb. The thumb of someone who was choking her to death."

Keith made a disgruntled noise and threw up his hands. "Now she's Columbo. Brilliant, Jamie, just brilliant. Next you'll have everyone in the county up in arms, beating the bushes looking for a psychotic killer."

But the look on Roman's face indicated that he was giving Jamie's theory some serious thought. In brooding silence he studied the mark again, his jaw muscles working. Meanwhile Jamie started feeling a little dizzy, overwhelmed by the mental act of lending truth to such a horrendous possibility. Fearing she might faint, she moved back to one of the front pews and sat down, staring blankly at the pink satin bow centered in the flower arrangement at the foot of the casket. Keith followed her cue and sat down in the pew across the aisle, his eyes focused upward on the large wooden cross hanging behind the pulpit, as if praying for Jamie to receive the other half of her brain.

Roman finally turned from the casket to look at Jamie, his shoulders slumped. "I doubt if anyone else would believe it, especially since Danica signed that stupid-ass letter I thought up, but that's really the only thing that would make any sense to me. She wasn't suicidal."

"You two are building quite a little bomb," Keith warned.

"Shut up, Keith." Resting her elbows on her knees, Jamie bent forward to cradle her chin in her upturned palms. Electrified as her system presently was, she still thought she would fall sound asleep if she closed her eyes for more than a second. "You heard Tommy threaten to kill her with your own ears."

"But Tommy threatens to kill everybody that twirks him off," Keith grumbled. "And if you'll remember, you've said you were gonna kill me a couple of times. I'm telling you, Jamie, you're blowing this all out of proportion. Don't you think Sheriff Hammond can tell the difference between a person who's been strangled manually and one who's been hanged?"

The look she gave him in response required no words.

"Well, the coroner, then. He had to sign her death certificate."

Ignoring him, Jamie said to Roman, "I think we'd better go have a talk with our illustrious sheriff, don't you? We can be back in time for the funeral."

Roman nodded. His former expression of grief had been replaced by one of barely controlled anger. "Okay, let's go. You coming, Keith?"

Keith slid sullenly down in the pew and shook his head.

Striding through the vestibule toward the front doors, Roman and Jamie encountered Alan, who had just stumbled in. He was wearing a navy suit and white cotton shirt, unbuttoned to the center of his hairless chest, no tie, instead of his usual fall attire of faded jeans with shredded knees and an extra-large flannel shirt or sweatshirt bearing some rebellious insignia, but the suit was wrinkled and disheveled and his breath reeked of liquor.

"Sorry I'm late. Couldn't 'member where I'd put the keys to my truck."

Jamie wasn't surprised. Sometimes Alan forgot where he'd left his truck. "Keith's in the chapel. Go on in and sit down before you fall down. We'll be back in a little while."

"Where ya goin'?" Alan queried, blasting them both with eye-watering fumes as he fought to keep his balance.

Pulling out of his breathing range, Jamie nodded toward the open doors of the chapel. "Whew. Never mind. Just get in there before Fred comes out and sees you. Keith knows where we're going. You can ask him."

And with that, Jamie skirted Alan's unsteady bulk and hurried for the exit with Roman in tow. Outside, the sun which had been shining with irreverent brilliance when she and Keith had arrived was now appropriately hidden behind a large gray pillow of clouds.

Chapter Five

By the time they finally tracked down Sheriff
Hammond at the Ace Cafe, Jamie and Roman
had convinced themselves beyond the shadow of
a doubt that Tommy Davidson had murdered
Danica for hitting him in the head with her
purse. An inner voice kept telling Jamie that this
was just too absurd, too unreal to be believed,
but she stopped listening when she realized the
voice belonged to her father, to whom all things
adolescent were absurd. She didn't believe he had
ever been a teenager. He'd been hatched in a bank
vault at the age of thirty.

Hank Hammond was slouched comfortably in
one of the rear booths across from his faithful
sidekick Pete Dudley. On the dull red Formica
table between them sat two cups of steaming coffee, a stack of dirty plates, and a gold aluminum
ashtray awaiting more ashes from Hank's smelly
cigar.

They were laughing when Jamie and Roman

strode purposefully up to their table; Hank was always telling jokes, and Pete always laughed whether they were funny or not, which was probably the reason he had the uncoveted privilege of hanging out with the sheriff. This being the day of Danica's funeral, Jamie felt like slapping them both.

Still chuckling, Hank peered up at Jamie through the gray smoke spiraling from the tip of his cigar. "How do, young lady. Somethin' I can do for you?"

After glancing at Roman for a dose of moral support, Jamie nodded, aware that her entire body was trembling. Suddenly it felt like every pore was yielding an ocean of sweat. "I want you to arrest Tommy Davidson for murder."

Hank looked at Pete, then back up at Jamie. The expression on his Uncle Fester face clearly showed what he was thinking. Paranoid schizophrenia. But Hank probably didn't know those fancy fifty-cent words. He just thought she was nuts.

"Say what?"

Jamie wondered if she was going to have to draw him a picture. "Tommy Davidson killed Danica Hooker. He said he was going to in front of about twenty witnesses, including Roman here, and he wasn't at school yesterday. And there's a suspicious bruise on Danica's neck. It couldn't have been caused by the rope. We think he choked her, then hung her to make it look like she'd committed suicide. He must have heard about that letter she signed, and saw his opportunity."

Suddenly there was silence and Jamie thought of the saying, 'You could have heard a pin drop', or, as Alan would probably say, you could have heard a gnat fart. There were several other patrons sitting at other tables, and Jamie could practically hear their ears stretching to catch her every word. Oops. She should have kept her voice down.

Sheriff Hammond slowly removed the fat cigar from his mouth and tapped the ashes absently into the aluminum tray. "Miss Fox, here's what I think," he responded in his famous Emperor of the Universe tone. "I think you've been sitting in front of the boob tube way too much. Murder just don't happen in this town. Now why don't you and Roman run along and go buy yourselves a sody pop or somethin'. Forget this cockeyed idea of yours, 'cause that's what it is."

His reaction was pretty much what Jamie had expected. If her and Roman's charge turned out to be true, Hank Hammond would look like an idiot, having told the *Deer Creek Review* that there had been absolutely no sign of foul play. He knew it as well as she, so he wasn't about to investigate the matter and in so doing make a complete fool of himself.

"Did you even see the bruise I'm talking about, Sheriff?"

"Danica and I were very close," Roman piped up, standing straight with his sparrow's chest thrust out. There was no way a skinny little runt like him could intimidate a man with the girth of a semi, but Jamie was impressed by his attempt. "And I know for a fact that she wasn't suicidal. If it came down to it, she wouldn't have given herself an Indian burn to save the old depot. That letter she signed, that five of us signed, was a total farce and we all knew it. You have to at least talk to Tommy. Find out if he can account for yesterday."

Hammond's froggy eyes narrowed. "Just where do you get off tellin' me what to do, squirt? Now you two skee-daddle before you get my dander up. You do that, you're likely to be sorry."

Jamie sighed in defeat. It would be easier to drive a wet noodle through granite than it would be to get the possibility of murder in Deer Creek into the sheriff's pea of a brain. "Come on, Roman, let's go. The funeral starts in seven minutes."

"A gold ring in a pig's ear does not a princess make," Roman quoted officiously at Hank before doing a crisp about-face to follow Jamie out of the cafe, past the wide-eyed diners who were obviously itching to repeat what they'd heard. Jamie flashed them all a wide pretentious smile below glaring eyes. Sheriff Hammond loudly demanded an explanation for whatever it was Roman had said, but neither turned or gave a reply, leaving him to figure it out for himself.

* * *

Talk about audacity. Jamie couldn't believe Tommy Davidson had the nerve to show up for the funeral. And not only had he shown up, he'd chosen to sit right on the front row, across the aisle from Danica's family. But giving it a little more thought, she decided that his actions made sense in a coldly logical way. He was taking great care to look perfectly innocent. She could hardly stand to look at him, thinking about what he'd done.

The chapel was nearly packed, most of the faces familiar. One of them belonged to the mayor. Jamie couldn't stand to look at him, either. Up front, the casket was now closed, the upper lid covered by a spray of white roses. Standing in the aisle, Jamie scanned the pews for Keith and Alan, finding them on the far end of the right rear pew. The back of Alan's head was tilted against the oak-paneled wall, eyes closed, mouth gaping open. Passed out. Jamie shook her head sadly.

Suddenly she felt a burst of pity for Alan, while at the same time feeling helpless. She wished there was *something* she could do to help him with his problems. But what could she do? Certainly things would get better for Alan once he got away from his parents and went off to college, but that wouldn't be for another year. And at this rate, if he kept drinking the way he was, eventually he would wind up dead, either behind the wheel of his car or because of his health. The last thing she wanted was to lose another friend.

Maybe she could talk to Keith and Roman about Alan's drinking and they could work together and try to help him. Maybe get him into some sort of program. She'd known Alan since they were five years old, and she wasn't going to stand by helplessly like she did with Danica.

Feeling someone's gaze on her from the other side of the chapel, she looked to her left and promptly discovered the accuracy of her intuition. The sensation of low-voltage electricity racing up her arms and meeting at the nape of her neck made her shudder slightly, but with pleasure. It was Morey. Jamie noticed that his mother was sitting between him and his father, with Malcolm at the aisle end of the pew. There was room for at least three people on Morey's left, and with a discreet nod of his head, Morey invited Jamie to occupy some of it.

As if she needed her arm twisted to force her into it, Jamie first reaffirmed that the pew on which Keith and Alan were sitting/sleeping was already too crowded, and of all the remaining seating space, the one next to Morey was the most convenient.

Nudging Roman she whispered, "Come on, I see a place." She didn't look back to see Keith's reaction when she settled herself right next to Morey, making Roman maneuver past another set of knees, but she guessed he was probably having a cow. She didn't care. Served him right for calling her a nerfbrain and treating her just as badly as that big buffoon behind a sheriff's badge had.

"This is really depressing," Morey muttered softly from the corner of his mouth.

Jamie lowered her head and began fidgeting with the zipper of her buckskin jacket. This was depressing, all right, ultimately so, but Jamie was also experiencing what she could only describe as ultimate euphoria, although the combination of such opposite emotions in one person at the same time shouldn't be possible. "She was my best friend. I'm really going to miss her."

"You know anything about that paper the sheriff mentioned?" Morey whispered, leaning close enough for Jamie to get a whiff of an exotic, musky cologne. "Was that for real?"

Jamie didn't answer, seeing that the service was about to begin. The pastor of First Southern Baptist, Kermit "the Frog" Pollard, solemnly passed their pew wearing a charcoal gray suit that looked two sizes too big and carrying a Bible that had to weigh fifty pounds. The organ music faded away, and in its wake the silence was filled with the rustling of fabrics, sniffling, and occasional throat-clearings. After making a variety of woeful expressions toward the ceiling, Pastor Pollard opened his massive Bible on the pulpit and began the eulogy by reading Psalm 23.

Jamie heard the words "The Lord is my Shepherd, I shall not want," but after that, her mind tuned to a different channel, the How To Get Tommy Busted channel. She stared at the back of his head wishing she could hear what was going on inside. Was he laughing behind his mask of grief? Was he scared that he still might get caught?

She was working on her umpteenth sting operation when Morey nudged her and asked in a low whisper, "You want to go out and get a Coke after the burial service?"

There was going to be a reception afterward at the Masons' lodge, but Jamie wasn't very hot on going to it. It appalled her that people could even think of eating after attending a funeral. What she really wanted to do was go straight home after this service ended, fall into bed, and sleep dreamlessly for at least a week. Right now, that sounded like heaven. But so did going out with Morey for a Coke. Eenie, meenie, miney . . .

To heck with sleep, she could do that anytime. "Sure," she whispered back, suppressing the hippopotamus smile that threatened to break out on her face. Morey had asked her out on a Coke date! Had she already fallen asleep on the pew and was only dreaming this? No, it was real. And oh, what juicy fodder for the Deer Creek rumor mill — possible romance involving the dashing young future politician Morey Monroe. Aside from Danica's untimely death, a chewier chunk of gossip could not be hoped for. Poor Danica would too soon be forgotten. But only until Jamie brought her killer to justice. Maybe Morey could help. Then again, unlike her, he probably wouldn't dare do anything that might reflect badly on his politically ambitious father.

When the chapel service was concluded, Jamie

quietly informed Roman of her plan to leave with Morey after the burial. Roman didn't say anything, but she could see by the look in his eyes that he didn't approve. Pretending not to notice, she gave him a wan smile and leaned over to plant a kiss on his cheek. "In case I miss Keith outside, tell him for me, okay?" By all means Jamie intended to avoid Keith, afraid he might do or say something embarrassing in front of Morey.

Roman's eyes darted to the front of the chapel, the disapproval in them turning to hate. His frown deepened. "What about Tommy? What are we gonna do?"

"I'll call you later," Jamie promised. "Don't worry, we'll get the bastard somehow."

In Deer Creek, the only places that sold fountain drinks were the drug store, Dairy Queen, and the Ace Cafe, but the cafe was strictly old-fogey territory. Morey let Jamie choose, and she opted for the Dairy Queen.

Settling into a back booth, Jamie was still haunted by the memory of watching Danica's casket get lowered by hydraulics into the ground. As was customary in that area, all the mourners tossed in a handful of dirt, and Jamie's imagination had cruelly summoned an image of Danica being awakened by the pattering sound and wondering where she was.

"You look tired."

Jamie jumped slightly at the sound of Morey's

voice. "Oh, yeah, well, I didn't get much sleep last night."

"That's understandable." Morey leaned back in the corner of the booth with his large Dr. Pepper, biting the end of his straw, intently exploring Jamie's face with his dark eyes. "So what about this paper thing, you never did answer me. Were you one of the four other knuckleheads?"

A corner of Jamie's mouth involuntarily curved upward, forming a small, crooked smile. "I plead the Fifth."

In the awkward silence that followed, Jamie's gaze wandered over to the pickup counter, now being vigorously polished by assistant manager Nancy Leibelle, a poor wheat farmer's widow. The woman had to be at least sixty years old, and the unflattering lines on her face suggested that her life hadn't exactly been a bed of roses. Just a few wild daisies, maybe, among an abundance of wicked thorns. In the back of her mind, Jamie heard her father's voice, ominous and certain like the ghost of Christmas future. *Take a good look, that's you in another forty years or so!*

Snapping back to the present, she realized that Morey had left the booth to put some quarters in the juke box. While he was still punching in his selections, Jon Bon Jovi's "Blaze of Glory" began to play, and Jamie felt an inner rush of tingly warmth. A man after her own heart.

After he returned to the table, Morey sipped at his Dr. Pepper for a few moments, then turned to gaze thoughtfully out the plate-glass window.

More dark clouds had gathered, casting a depressing fall gloom over the dying land below. A similar gloom had subtly claimed Morey's expression. "Don't repeat this to anybody, but my dad told me to find out all I could about it; to be honest, he almost did backflips when he read that article. Now, don't get the wrong idea—he felt very badly about Danica committing suicide—but he couldn't help but realize the political implications, how it might be used to blow Mayor Shepherd out of the saddle. You see, for my dad, the mayor's office is only a stepping-stone. He wants to go all the way. And I do mean *all* the way. To the very top."

Jamie's eyes widened. "You mean President?"

Without looking at her, Morey nodded solemnly.

"Wow." While that information was sinking in, Jamie became aware of another fact, a rather dismal fact: Morey had just confessed an ulterior motive for asking her out. He wasn't really interested in her, just in what she could tell him about the damn suicide pact. But she didn't want to believe that, and her mind obligingly coughed up a good reason why she shouldn't—the wink he'd given her in class Monday morning, when all anybody knew about Danica was her ordinary absence from school.

Now that it didn't matter, Jamie didn't mind telling him the details of what the five of them had done at the old depot on Saturday. Morey listened attentively as she spoke, seeming to mentally record every word for later playback for his father.

She finished by saying, "Your dad won't like this part, but Danica didn't kill herself because of that letter, or for any other reason. I'm reasonably sure she was murdered."

A shocked expression jumped on Morey's face. *"Murdered?"*

"Yes. I know who did it, too. And I'm going to see that he pays if it's the last thing I do."

"But the sheriff said—"

"Sheriff Hammond couldn't find his own butt with both hands and a flashlight," Jamie muttered angrily. "Take anything he says with a grain of salt. I know what I know. All I have to do now is figure out some way to prove it."

From the corner of her eye she saw another vehicle pulling into the lot beside Morey's Ferrari. Taking a better look, she immediately recognized Keith's battered pickup. Alan was sitting shotgun, his appearance a good advertisement for all drug- and alcohol-dependency treatment clinics.

Jamie groaned. "Oh no. Here comes trouble."

Morey glanced over his shoulder. "Is Keith Maguire your boyfriend? I didn't think—"

"No, just a friend, but he has been acting a little weird lately," Jamie sighed. "Kinda possessive or something. I don't know, I try not to think about it. He's been like a brother to me for a long time, since we were little kids." She had a sudden urge to duck out the back door, but none of her weary body parts seemed able to move.

Morey didn't seem too concerned. Maybe he did have a black belt in karate—not that he'd need one to knock Alan over. A good gust of wind would probably do it for him, Jamie thought as she watched her fellow knuckleheads emerge from the pickup's cab.

"So, how long are you going to keep me in suspense?" Morey had refocused his attention on her, his dark eyes now exuding unbridled impatience.

It took Jamie a moment to figure out what he was talking about. She was hesitant at first to relinquish such sensitive information, but then she remembered that several locals had overheard her telling Sheriff Hammond in the cafe. So it was only a matter of time before he would find out anyway. "The circumstances point to Tommy Davidson. Weren't you at the depot Saturday night? Didn't you see the fight?"

His eyes flashed with remembrance. "Oh yeah. Danica snuck up behind him while he was bent over rabbit-punching Roman's kidneys and knocked him down with her purse. He said he was going to kill her."

"And he kept his word." Jamie's face hardened as her mind produced a vision of Tommy smiling triumphantly as he choked the life out of her best friend. Nobody hits Tommy Davidson in the head with a purse and gets away with it.

Then Keith and Alan entered through the west door and approached the order counter, vanquishing the horrid mental scene. Jamie tensed, preparing for the two to come over but it didn't take her long to realize they were both carefully ignoring her. Not once did either of them so much as glance in the direction of her and Morey's booth. How childish, she thought. How utterly juvenile. They were all seniors now, supposedly one step away from adulthood. Keith and Alan were acting like sixth graders. But actually she was glad they were ignoring her and Morey. They very well could be acting like Neanderthal cavemen instead. Both had quite a talent for it, as she well knew.

Not wishing to push her luck, she glanced down at her wristwatch, then gave Morey an apologetic smile. "I need to be getting home. My jailers let me out to attend the funeral, but officially I'm grounded."

Smiling back at her with slanted eyes, Morey finished his Dr. Pepper with a loud slurp, then crushed the paper cup in his hand. Curling his other hand into a fist, he brought it to his mouth to stymie a soft belch. "What did you do?"

Jamie didn't want to tell him she was grounded for sneaking Keith into the house after her parents had gone to bed while she was grounded for driving like a maniac, and her sleep-deprived brain was presently unable to think up a good white lie. "Don't ask," she said dryly.

Morey shrugged and let the subject drop. "Okay, let's go. I'll take you home."

They walked past the counter where Keith was giving his order to Nancy Leibelle and to which Alan was clinging for support. They were still pointedly keeping their eyes averted from her and Morey's vicinity. She thought about saying hi to them, an adult thing to do, she thought, but her lips remained sealed. If that didn't start something, it would give them an opportunity to really be snotty by not responding. She would then be obliged to call them both on the phone and hang up on them without saying anything at least three times apiece.

On the way to her house, all she could think about was whether or not Morey was planning to kiss her when he dropped her off. She was afraid to hope too much, since it seemed that wanting things really bad sometimes sent a secret signal to the Universe to make sure you didn't get it. She hoped anyway. Mainly she didn't want to spend the solitary hours ahead worrying that he'd only used her to get information for his dad. She'd much rather spend it reliving over and over the electric moment their lips and tongues had met. Remembering the way he'd said something like, "I'll call you later, you foxy Fox." Gazing at the class ring he'd slipped on her finger.

"Well, here you are. Guess I'll see you tomorrow."

Pop went Jamie's lovely balloon. She looked over at him with an alluring, pouty, kiss-me-you-fool expression she'd practiced countless times in front of her mirror, reaching slowly, very slowly, for the door handle. "Thanks for the ride. And the Coke." Her sultriest voice. Another voice inside her head was ranting vehemently, *"Don't be a jerk! Take me, I'm yours! Puleeeease!"*

"My pleasure," he said formally. "We'll have to do it again sometime when you're not grounded." Morey's fingers tapped against the steering wheel, an indication that he wanted to be on his way. Apparently her time card had been punched the moment he pulled in front of her parents' house.

Jamie hid her disappointment well. She'd practiced a few other meaningful expressions, and one of them said, "I'll pencil you into my heavy schedule, but don't hold your breath, peasant." She put it on and said coolly, "Yeah, sure, whatever."

Not until she was safely behind her closed front door did she allow her true emotions to show. At first she was angry for the way that Morey had treated her. But then her anger turned to tears as she realized that today she had said good-bye to her best friend and she would never see her again. And although there was nothing she could do to change what had happened to Danica, there was one thing she could do. And she would.

She would find her best friend's murderer.

Chapter Six

The house was completely dark, silent and cold as the grave. She was crouched down in her closet, shivering, hiding, each beat of her heart a scream of terror. Her exhaled breaths seemed loud as cannon blasts in the enclosed space. She tried to breathe quietly, but her fear made it impossible. She prayed he wouldn't come close enough to hear. He was in the house. She knew it for certain; she'd heard the tinkling of broken glass, the creak of the utility-room door being opened. He was here to silence her forever. He couldn't allow her to stir up trouble. No, Tommy couldn't have that. And he knew just what to do about it because she'd signed the letter too.

When he killed her he'd make it look like another suicide.

She should never have told him she had proof. That had been her worst mistake. She should have gone directly to Sheriff Bumpkin. Seeing her evidence, even the moronic likes of him would have been forced to admit there was something very rotten in Deer Creek. But now he'd just have to think up some other way of covering his lazy ass.

It was the Nikki Sixx bass guitar pick that Danica's older sister Erica had sent her from Houston for her sixteenth birthday. Last night Jamie had gone to sleep remembering that she'd overheard Darlene asking her mother at the graveside service where the pick was; she'd searched all through Danica's room the night before and hadn't been able to find it. And Mrs. Hooker had answered that she didn't know, she never paid any attention to such items. The pick was one of Danica's most prized possessions. The band Mötley Crüe, to whom Danica was a devoted fan, would throw these things out into the audience during or after a concert. Danica's pick was embossed with the bass guitarist's name, Nikki Sixx, but what made it most valuable, of course, was the fact that he had probably actually *touched* it with his own bare hand. The first time Danica had lifted it from the cotton batting on which it was nestled like the rarest jewel on Earth, she swore she could hear a host of angels singing the "Hallelujah Chorus."

A place for everything and everything in its place. In Danica's room, that applied only to the Nikki Sixx pick; everything else was thrown helter-skelter. There was an open shelf in the headboard of her sagging double bed, and in the center of that shelf lay a large red heart edged with lace that she'd cut from an old box of Valentine candy. In an inner pink heart sat the small white jeweler's box that contained the pick.

It was never anywhere else. Ever, unless Danica had taken it out to fondle it and dream of being up on that pulsating stage with Mötley Crüe, hammered by multicolored lights as she danced next to Nikki Sixx, awaiting her cue to take the microphone. Danica had been a little weird.

The fact that it was gone kept nagging at Jamie. She couldn't imagine Danica putting it somewhere else. Yet Darlene had said she'd looked thoroughly. Danica wouldn't have given it away, either. Hardly. She probably wouldn't have taken a thousand dollars for it. But it couldn't have walked off by itself . . .

And then Jamie knew. Tommy had taken it. It was a stupid move, possibly the one fatal flaw in an otherwise perfect plan, but the temptation had proved irresistible. Perhaps he'd deluded himself into thinking it wouldn't be missed.

There was a soft creak of flooring nearby, and Jamie pressed herself deeper into the shadows, clamping her hands tightly over her mouth. Her heart was thumping so madly she feared it would burst.

Another creak. The sound of a switch being flipped. A thin strip of light glared through the center of the closet doors and at the bottom. A thin squeal rose in Jamie's throat, but she managed to keep it in.

There was some shuffling, followed by a dark throaty chuckle. He'd figured out where she was.

Then the doors were flung open, and there he was, a huge menacing shadow framed in bright blurry light. Tommy came closer, leaning over to sneer at her. "Come on, Jamie. We're through playing hide-and-seek. Now it's time to play suicide."

He was reaching for her, his face a mask of cruel glee. He was going to enjoy this, just as he'd enjoyed doing it to Danica. Jamie began releasing all the screams she'd been holding back, kicking at him and trying to claw his hand with her fingernails, but he only laughed, and soon managed to grab one of her ankles. With one brutal motion, he yanked her out of the closet.

Then suddenly the light went out —

Jamie opened her eyes to find herself thrashing wildly at her covers. It took several moments for her to realize she'd just had another nightmare, a few minutes more to completely calm down. Looking at the glowing digits on her clock, she saw that it was almost nine P.M. After Morey Monroe's Ferrari had roared off down the street, she dried her tears, had dinner with her parents and then went to bed, having fallen asleep almost immediately.

Still a bit shaken from the nightmare, she reached over to turn on her bedside lamp. The light made her feel a little safer. Her stomach made a growling noise, but other than that, the house seemed devoid of its usual evening sounds: a television program, muffled voices in conversation, the thunks and scrapes of human activity.

Her parents must have gone out. She knew they wouldn't be in bed this early. That only happened on their anniversary.

She found a note downstairs, pinned by a magnet to the refrigerator where she would be sure to see it. The note, written in her mother's precise, flowing script, informed her that they had gone over to the Woodleys' and would be home around ten. It also reminded her that she was grounded and not allowed to leave the house or to have any of her friends over. Jamie jerked the refrigerator door open and scanned the shelves for something to eat, thinking that her parents never got home from the Woodleys' before eleven. She remembered her and Jefferson being dragged to those little get-togethers when they were younger. While the adults drank and played cards or some other stupid game like Trivial Pursuit or drank and watched football in the den, Jamie and Jefferson and the two Woodley kids, left to their own devices, usually demolished the rest of the house. That part was always fun, but invariably they were forced to put everything back in order, and that had always been the ultimate drag.

She removed a covered yellow Tupperware container from the third shelf in hopes of finding something edible inside. Yechhh. Penicillin culture on some leftover meatloaf. Good Lord, it had been at least two weeks since they'd had meatloaf for dinner. If her mom didn't like to play peek-a-boo, she ought to put dates on these things. Grimacing, Jamie tossed the container in the kitchen sink.

Peek-a-boo. Hide-and-seek. The nightmare.

Tommy Davidson.

A slight shiver ran the length of Jamie's body. The Nikki Sixx pick and its disappearance had not been a product of her imagination. She really had overheard Darlene at the graveside ceremony asking her mother where it was, saying she'd looked all over and hadn't been able to find it. But Jamie hadn't said anything about it to anyone else yet, least of all Tommy.

The sight of the grody meatloaf had effectively quelled her appetite. She closed the refrigerator door and stared at her mother's note without really seeing it. If she could find the Nikki Sixx pick in Tommy's possession, that should provide ample evidence of his guilt. It certainly wasn't the sort of item he could have picked up at the local thrift store. To Jamie's knowledge, Danica had been the only local teenager in possession of one. Surely Jamie would have heard if there was another. A prize like that pick came with an unlimited license to brag. Unless of course it came as ill-gotten booty. As a reward for murder.

"Remember, you're to stay home, and no company."

Her father had confiscated her car keys, but Jamie had an extra set that he didn't know about. Even if her parents planned to return when the note said, she still had the better part of an hour to do a little sleuthing. That guitar pick had to be somewhere in Tommy Davidson's personal living quarters, an efficiency apartment converted from the one-car garage attached to his parents' house—Jamie suspected Mr. and Mrs. Davidson had done this to preserve their own sanity. Tommy would want the new treasure to be handy, so he could take it out and look at it as often as he liked, perhaps fantasize that he was Nikki Sixx, idol to millions of teenage girls, and use the pick to skillfully play an air guitar along with his *Dr. Feelgood* tape. The idea made Jamie want to vomit.

She hurried upstairs for her shoes and her secret set of car keys, telling herself not to think about what she was doing, just do what had to be done. She couldn't allow Tommy to get away with his crime. If she did, she'd wouldn't be able to live with herself.

Five minutes later, Jamie was cruising slowly toward Tommy's house on the east side of town, carefully obeying all traffic rules to avoid getting a ticket that would definitely nail her for going AWOL. She wondered uneasily how she was going to weasel her way into Tommy's apartment and conduct a surreptitious search without arousing his suspicion. Knowing that she had been Danica's best friend, he would automatically be on guard, but perhaps she could somehow put him at ease. Make him think she wanted to apply for the new girlfriend position, now that Lisa Gayle was out of the picture. It would be a tough role to play convincingly, very tough considering the fact that she'd like nothing better than to throw him into the mouth of an active volcano, but she couldn't think of anything better.

Now another worry was added to increase Jamie's tension; it seemed that someone was following her, but all she could see of the other vehicle in her rearview mirror were its headlights piercing the foggy gloom. Just please don't let it be my parents, she prayed silently, certain that whoever was back there could easily make out her incriminating personalized license plate: JAMIE. Only one of those in town, eliminating all guesswork. Good-bye, car. But several moments after she turned onto Mulberry Lane where Tommy lived, the mysterious beams of light continued straight along Twelfth Street.

Jamie breathed a sigh of relief, taking her eyes from the rearview mirror to peer at the dark row of small tract houses on her right. In the light of day they were pretty, homey little places graced with plenty of trees, mostly willows, evergreens, and maples, the clapboard exteriors painted a variety of pastel colors. These were, by and large, the homes of the blue-collar paper-mill employees. But now, shrouded in the heavy darkness of a moonless night and the diaphanous clinging fog, Jamie thought they looked as creepy as ancient mausoleums inhabited by the living dead. Then she immediately warned herself to stop thinking like that before she scared herself right into hot-rodding it for home.

The Davidsons lived in the sixth house down the block. There was one other house on the north side of it before Mulberry dead-ended. The front of the garage had been bricked up, except for the small window space, which made it a strange cousin to all its strictly wooden neighbors. So there was no question in Jamie's mind as to whether or not she had the right house. The oil-stained, unoccupied front curb and empty driveway told her that the murderous fiend was not at home. Tommy drove an old blue Camaro that looked like it had been in a few demolition derbies. Actually it had only been in one, but for that Tommy was no less proud.

At first Jamie felt defeated, left with nothing to do but go back home and stew about her thwarted mission. Or mope about getting used by Morey. Then she noticed through the fog a light behind the curtains of the picture window over the front porch. Someone was home. Had to be one of Tommy's parents.

Did she dare?

She dared. Pulling to a stop in front of the next house down and dousing her headlights, it felt like her body was on autopilot. Her stomach made a loud rope-twisting noise as she turned off the ignition, and she silently commanded it to shut up, she didn't need its unqualified opinion. This could turn out to be a truly deluxe opportunity. It might be her one chance to search for the Nikki Sixx pick without Tommy around.

It was Tommy's father who answered the door,

a Bud Lite clutched in his right hand, his stolid face darkened with stubble.

Raising her voice to compete with the country-music video blaring from the television behind him, Jamie dredged up a smile and half-shouted, "I'm looking for Tommy. Do you know where he went or when he'll be back?"

Wes Davidson craned his neck to look over her head at the empty street out front. "Thought he was here, so I don't know."

Now for the clincher. Jamie hoped she wasn't blowing it by asking permission. Hearing a no wouldn't necessarily crush her plan, but plan B was a lot scarier, and especially disastrous if she got caught. In legalese, she believed the term was *breaking and entering.* For that, her father would break down and enter her into a girl's boarding school with an innocuous name like Whitefern or Springbrook Academy but would undoubtedly be surrounded by razor wire and run by a wicked headmistress. Never mind that she had a very noble excuse for committing her dastardly deed, to see that a cold-blooded killer was brought to justice. Nor would it matter that countless TV and movie detectives had provided a bad example by bending the rules to suit their purposes.

"Well, ah, you think it would be okay if I waited for him in his room? He probably just went to get a Coke or something. I'm sure he wouldn't mind." She looked up at him with her most angelic, trustworthy expression. It didn't work on her dad anymore, but Wes Davidson hardly knew her.

He shrugged. "Don't make no difference to me. Side door's probably locked, though, so you'll have to go through the door off the kitchen." He opened the screen door and pointed with his beer can. "Watch your step in there, usually looks like a tornado's been through it."

Jamie responded with a gratuitous laugh that sounded as phony as it was, but she doubted Mr. Davidson had noticed; he was already resettled in his Barcalounger, his attention devoted to Reba McIntire.

Proceeding to the kitchen, Jamie's pulse jumped from high gear to warp speed. How much time did she have before Tommy returned?

Just as Wes Davidson had warned, Tommy's living quarters looked like a tornado had been through there. And Jamie had thought Danica was a slob. She'd never seen such a mess. Maybe she'd be able to find a hidden Volkswagen in here, but finding the quarter-sized pick would be next to impossible.

She was tempted to wade her way over to the side door and leave, give up the crusade for legal justice, and figure out some other way to make Tommy suffer for the rest of his life. Taking the pick was very risky, so it had to mean a great deal to him. He wouldn't just toss it on the floor where it could easily be lost among the discarded clothes and other junk. Unless he was carrying it on his person, he most likely would have put it away in a safe place, like a drawer or cache box or cookie jar.

All four walls and the ceiling of the rectangular room were covered with giant posters—heavy-metal bands interspersed with tanned beauties in string bikinis straddling motorcycles (utterly gross)—and the air smelled of stale sweat and beer. On one end was a filthy kitchenette and bathroom, in the middle a decrepit couch, three bean-bag cushions, a small television sitting on an unvarnished cable spool, and of course the music equipment and accessories no teenager could live without. On the far end was the elevated waterbed and a pile of clothes in the shape of a dresser.

Assuming Tommy's mentality, which made her want to swing from trees and eat bananas, she asked herself which of the three areas she would choose to hide her small treasure. Her eyes slowly gravitated toward the stereo setup. A logical correlation: guitar pick—stereo. Both made music, and Jamie noticed that the tops of both upright speaker boxes were crammed with rummage-sale specials, among them a ceramic cobra in a coiled striking pose, Buddha incense burner, and a small plastic toilet that squirted water at the person stupid enough to lift the lid when Tommy told them to. He'd taken it to the depot one night the previous summer and the stream had gotten Jamie right in the eye.

Taking care where she stepped in case Tommy had planted land mines around the room for security, she slowly approached the entertainment area. Through the wall on her right she could hear the country tune being broadcast from the television in the living room. It made Jamie thankful that her parents weren't great music lovers, because they'd probably be into some really horrible stuff like Glen Miller or Frank Sinatra. But mostly it made Jamie worry that she wouldn't hear Tommy's car drive up.

Her hand trembled as she bent to pick up the ceramic cobra, thinking it might be hollow with an open bottom. Her assumption proved correct, but a look inside told her the pick wasn't hidden in there. She carefully returned it to the exact same spot, clearly outlined by a layer of dust. Still trembling, her hand moved on to the next item, the incense burner.

Please please please. She held her breath as she picked it up, but the Buddha had a solid bottom and there was nothing underneath it but a squashed candy wrapper. Strike two.

She eyed the toilet warily. Surely not. But then, wouldn't that be perfect? Everyone who knew Tommy also knew what happened when the toilet's lid was lifted, so what idiot was going to lift it? Taking it carefully from the speaker, she had a spine-tingling vision of the Nikki Sixx pick lying down in the plastic bowl. Proof positive that she had not, as Sheriff Bozo had accused, been watching too much of the boob tube. He was the boob, and this little baby was going to make her a local heroine.

Jamie lifted the small brown lid and was

promptly squirted—not with tapwater, but with rancid beer. Some of it hit her chin, but the rest soaked into her favorite lavender and pink cashmere sweater. A small price to pay had the pick been down inside the bowl as she'd envisioned, but as her luck would have it, the bowl was empty.

Strike three. But now she was more angry than frightened, and if she had to tear this room—make that *clean this room*—until it looked like the fastidious Felix Unger from *The Odd Couple* lived here, she would, if that's what it took to find Danica's pick, because it *was* here, it simply had to be.

She was reaching for a small round wooden cache box that looked like something Tommy would have made in shop class when the curtains over the room's one window, which faced the driveway, suddenly flared with light. Jamie's heart leapt into her throat as fear recaptured control of her emotions. She insisted to herself that it was only Mrs. Davidson back from bowling or some civic meeting, there was no cause for alarm, but her parasympathetic nervous system wasn't listening. Torn between fight and flight, she stood frozen in total panic.

A car door opened, then slammed closed. Now footsteps coming up the drive. Jamie let out the breath she'd been subconsciously holding, convinced that the sound of those brisk footsteps were being made by pump heels, and no way on God's green earth would Tommy be wearing a pair of women's pumps. But her muscles remained tensed, pulse in overdrive. She could probably chalk this up to the most nerve-wracking experience of her life, except maybe for the time, at the age of ten, she'd been chased up a tree by one of Ernie Cobb's giant hogs.

After hearing the front door open and close and Mrs. Davidson bellow at her husband to turn down the television before it gave her a migraine, Jamie continued her search, her movements now fast and frantic. The cache box contained an assortment of screws, nails, and thumbtacks. No guitar pick. Jamie quickly replaced it on the speaker, disregarding the dust outline of its original position.

When she'd checked everything on the speakers and made a close inspection of the shelves housing the attached stereo equipment, she abandoned her music-with-music theory and went for the dresser, hastily transferring the clothes piled on it to the foot of the bed. There were six drawers, and they were all partially opened with more clothes hanging out every which way. Jamie wondered if there might be mice or rats living in them. All she needed now was to get bitten by one and have to worry about rabies or bubonic plague.

She was tentatively poking through the first one when she heard another set of footsteps coming up along the side of the garage. These were not made by pumps. These were definitely made by boots. Big cowboy boots.

Tommy was home.

In a flurry of panic, Jamie scooped up the clothes she'd piled on the foot of the waterbed and spread them back on the dresser top. There was no time to do anything else but plop herself onto one of the bean-bag cushions before Tommy opened the side door and stepped in. Apparently it had not been locked after all.

She tried to look cool, calm and collected, but knew that her heavy breathing and rapid jugular pulse was a dead giveaway that she'd been up to something. Remembering the nightmare she'd had earlier that evening brought a sudden lump to her throat. "Oh, hi, Tommy. What took you so long?"

He hadn't noticed her until she spoke; apparently she blended well with the surrounding disaster area. The surprise almost caused him to drop the Dairy Queen cup in his hand. "What are you doin' here?"

Deer Creek did not have a football team—they were big on basketball and track—but if they did, Tommy would have made an excellent offensive linebacker. His face was ugly enough to turn a train down a dirt road: badly pocked skin, the misshapen nose of a professional boxer (presently a bit swollen thanks to Alan) Cro-Magnon forehead. His collar-length brown hair was thin and stringy, and presently his eyes made her think of Norman Bates.

"What are you doing here?" he repeated, his tone laced with anger. He took another step closer, and Jamie's muscles went rigid in preparation for an assault.

"Your dad let me in. He said it would be okay if I waited for you back here." Jamie could hear the desperation in her voice, but there was nothing she could do about it. She was scared witless, being alone like this with Danica's murderer. Knowing that his parents were only a scream away wasn't much consolation. She might not get the chance to scream.

"I just came by to see you," she finished, trying to use as seductive a tone of voice as possible.

His eyes narrowed in suspicion, just as she'd feared they might. She and Tommy knew each other pretty well, but they'd never been what you would call friends. Naturally he would be suspicious.

"What for?" he asked brusquely, his gaze moving to sweep over his lair for evidence of unauthorized ransacking. It didn't take him long to find it on the stereo speakers where things had obviously been moved, according to the dust.

Filled with dread, Jamie had been following his gaze, and when it arrested on the stereo speakers, she knew she'd been had. *Our Father who art in Heaven* . . .

"You've been snoopin' around in my stuff," Tommy accused, turning to shove the door closed behind him. It clicked shut with a finality that send cold chills up Jamie's spine.

"Snooping?" She blinked her eyes innocently. "I was just *looking*. There's a difference, you know."

"Just looking. Yeah, right." Wearing a sneer that made him look as malevolent as a panther on the prowl, he took another step toward her, setting his Dairy Queen cup on top of the television set so he could place both hands on his hips. "I know exactly why you're here, I just wanted to see what you'd say. It's all over town you and Roman think I killed Danica and made it look like she'd hung herself."

Jamie hated to be caught in a lie, but she was far more concerned with her hide at this point than she was in her pride. She answered him in a trembling voice. "Well, you did threaten to kill her last Saturday night. Isn't that right?" Real, real bad time to smart off, she thought too late.

Tommy looked ready to give her a frontal lobotomy with his teeth. Leaning over, he growled down at her, "If I was really gonna kill somebody, I wouldn't make a public announcement about it. I'd just do it. How stupid do you think I am?"

Jamie thought it wise not to answer that. This seemed like a good time to scream for help. She opened her mouth, but nothing came out.

Tommy straightened, and his angry expression inexplicably mellowed. With the hint of a smile he almost looked pleasant, but there was an underlying sneakiness that Jamie didn't trust at all. She watched warily as he swaggered casually over to his stereo setup and pushed a button. The result was an instantaneous pounding flood of rock music through the speakers. It seemed he had read her mind. If she screamed now, she'd

124

hardly be able to hear herself.

Realization stabbed into her like a knife. He meant to do her bodily harm. Nothing fatal—at least one person, his father, knew she was here, and for all Tommy knew, she'd told half a dozen others she was coming. But what a glorious setup for another kind of violence. A redneck jerk like Tommy wouldn't dream of letting it go to waste. She'd asked for it, coming to his room all alone after dark. And the judge would probably agree.

Jamie scrambled out of the bean-bag cushion and backed away, glaring daggers at him. "Don't get any ideas, Tommy! I'm leaving right now!" She had to shout to be heard over the music.

"But I thought you came to see me, and I just got here!" Tommy began moving slowly toward her, dark lust shining in his deep-set feral eyes. His mouth was set in a thin cruel line.

Jamie found herself backed against the far wall, on the verge of a major freakout. To a large degree the nightmare had become reality. There was no waking up from this. She looked around frantically for some sort of defensive weapon. On the floor, between the right end of the dresser and the wall, was a steel jack—the spiky kind that came packaged by the dozen or so with a little red rubber ball—only this one was the size of a volleyball, another birthday or Christmas gift from Tommy's favorite uncle Jack, who owned a novelty store in Cincinnati. The spikes didn't look very sharp, but it was the best thing available. Tommy would hardly be threatened by a catcher's mitt.

Jamie grabbed it and held it out in front of her by one of the knobbed protrusions, dismayed that it wasn't nearly as heavy as it looked. "Stay away from me, Tommy! I'm not afraid to use this!"

At that he stopped and burst out laughing, which totally infuriated her. They would see who was laughing when one of these pointed spikes was shoved all the way up one of his nostrils. Still, she didn't feel brave enough to try forcing him backward, so she moved cautiously to the left, in the narrow space between the wall and the length of the waterbed, hoping Tommy would do the same. If he did, then she would have a semi-clear shot at the door. But she would have to move like greased lightning.

Wearing an evil smirk, Tommy continued his advance, and as Jamie had hoped, he cornered around the waterbed frame instead of cutting across the middle. Moving his two-hundred-plus pounds with languid ease, his smoldering stare promised pleasure — but it would all be his. The pain would all be hers.

Then Jamie saw it, on the wall behind him. For a moment she felt completely stupefied. Above and slightly to the left of Tommy's right shoulder was a large black-and-white Mötley Crüe poster, which was held in place by six thumbtacks — two on the top corners, two in the middle on the border, and two on the bottom corners. Arms crossed over a naked chest, the rest of his body squeezed into black leather, Nikki Sixx pouted back at her.

And the Nikki Sixx guitar pick she had come to find was pinned under the left middle thumbtack, bigger than daylight. The words were out before she could stop them. "Oh God, there it is."

His smirk fading, Tommy paused to glance over his shoulder. "What?"

"That proves it." A violent tremor ran through Jamie's body. She was really in trouble now. In another second he was going to realize what she had seen, and then he would have to kill her. He would have no choice.

His eyes fastened on the poster, Tommy made a slow retreat. As he reached for the pick, he looked back at her with a viciousness that froze her blood. After examining it for a few seconds, he held it up. "What's with this? It's not mine."

As if he had no idea. As if he wasn't lying by denying he had taken it from Danica's bedroom. Jamie swallowed, too scared to say a word.

Working the pick between his fingers, Tommy began to nod. "Oh, I see. This was Danica's, wasn't it? You came here to plant it on me, to make it look like I killed her!"

His accusation liberated her paralyzed vocal cords. "Oh, for sure! You took that from Danica's room and you know it! And you *did* kill her, you strangled her with your bare hands and—"

She didn't get to finish, because Tommy was coming for her, and this time he wasn't moving with languid ease. He was moving like a charging rhino. Indulging in a shrill scream whether it

127

would summon help or not, Jamie jumped up on the waterbed, intending to lumber across it and try to beat Tommy to the door. A good plan, but it didn't pan out. The lumbering turned into seriously uncoordinated stumbling, Tommy's waterbed being the old-fashioned kind without baffles. Tripped by a tidal wave, she went down very ungracefully, giving Tommy the opportunity to grab one of her ankles. Screaming louder, she kicked with her free leg and clung to the opposite side of the frame with her free hand, but Tommy was much stronger and had little trouble breaking her grip. His fingers dug into her calf like steel pincers as he pulled her back to the other side. Jamie caught a glimpse of his face as she continued to struggle for freedom with every ounce of adrenaline-hyped strength she possessed. His teeth were bared like a wolf's, his eyes the merciless black pools of a crocodile's. Tommy did not intend for her to leave this room alive. Jamie was certain that she was fighting for her very life.

He was pulling on her jacket now, attempting to turn her over on her back. The probable reason for this jolted her with a fresh wave of terror. If she was on her back, it would be easier for him to choke her. Acting on reflex, Jamie raised the giant jack and plunged the lowest spike as hard as she could into the back of Tommy's right hand.

He released her with a howl of pain just as the door leading to the kitchen swung open and Mrs. Davidson appeared in a quilted satin robe, a towel wrapped around her head and blue-green cream smeared all over her face. *"THOMAS HERSHALL DAVIDSON!! TURN DOWN THAT STEREO THIS INSTANT!!!"*

She had shouted this at the top of her lungs with her eyes closed, arms held rigidly at her sides and her hands balled into fists. Tommy's howl immediately degraded into a string of profanity muttered under his breath. Jamie wasted no time in taking advantage of her opportunity to scramble off the bed. Mrs. Davidson's eyes popped open like the Bride of Frankenstein's, her lips pursed tightly in anger. But when she saw Jamie, her expression changed to one of surprise and embarrassment.

"Oh, my! I didn't know you had company!"

"I was just leaving," Jamie said, and all but ran to the side door and let herself out, too afraid to take a parting look at Tommy's face. She could only imagine the rage he must be feeling over her getting away, especially after jabbing that spike into his hand. But he would catch up to her later, no doubt about that. And he would repay with interest.

Hurrying to her car, Jamie was so shaken she was amazed she could even walk. As she dug frantically for her car keys in her jeans pocket, she wondered what the chances were of her dad springing for an armed bodyguard. She'd never sleep again, worried that Tommy might be quietly cutting a screen on one of the downstairs windows.

And the pick. Tommy still had it, but he

wouldn't keep it now. He'd probably flush it down the toilet right away. So it would be her word against his. She knew the truth, but she couldn't prove it. Damn it to hell.

She was so nervous she accidentally stuck the ignition key into the door lock, realizing a split second too late that she hadn't even locked the stupid door. Frustration threatened to bring on tears as she tried to wriggle the key back out, muttering, "C'mon, c'mon, c'mon!" Not until she was behind the wheel with the doors locked and windows rolled up would she feel halfway safe. Any moment Tommy could come charging around the side of his house after her.

Finally the key pulled free without breaking off—Jamie was surprised it didn't, considering the way her luck usually ran—giving her frenzied nervous system a moderate injection of relief. She quickly pulled up the chrome handle and had the door open about a foot when she was suddenly grabbed from behind.

She emitted a shriek capable of shattering crystal and began kicking and flailing, grabbing for hair, ears, whatever might come off the easiest. Her attacker—she assumed it was Tommy—yelped when she yanked out a small tuft of hair and promptly released her. Jamie whirled around, ready to claw Tommy's murderous eyes out, but there stood Keith with his face screwed up in a grimace, vigorously rubbing the sore spot on his head.

"Man, you play rough!" he complained.

It took Jamie several seconds to catch her breath. Her heart was thumping so wildly against her ribcage she thought she was on the verge of having a heart attack. "Keith, don't you ever"— she paused to take a couple of deep breaths— "*ever* do that to me again. What are you doing here, anyway?"

Staring toward the dark open field beyond the dead-end sign, Keith continued to rub his head, wincing occasionally. While he was taking his sweet time answering, Jamie kept throwing nervous glances toward Tommy's house. The fact that Keith was there didn't offer much security. It would take three or four Keiths to equal the destructive force of one Tommy Davidson.

"Don't get mad," he said finally, "but I followed you over here from your parents' house. I was parked down the street with my lights off. But I wasn't spying on you, honest. I was afraid Tommy was going to try and do something to your car or to maybe even you, for starting that rumor about him. Roman told me what happened at the cafe, that some people overheard your conversation with the sheriff, and I knew what that meant. Anyway, then I saw you leave, and thought maybe I'd better follow in case you were planning to do something stupid like come over here and confront him."

Jamie didn't know whether to thank him or slap him. "So where were you when he was trying to choke me to death?"

Keith stopped rubbing his scalp, his mouth fall-

131

ing open like a landed trout's with eyes to match. "Tommy tried to *kill—?*"

"Well, he hadn't actually started choking me, but he was definitely working on it. And I'm sure he'll try again. I saw it, Keith. I saw Danica's Nikki Sixx pick up on Tommy's wall, tacked to a Mötley Crüe poster. That proves he killed her. That's the only way he could have gotten it."

Keith stood there looking dumbfounded.

"What have you got to say for yourself now, buster?" Jamie asked with a self-satisfied smirk. "Are you going to try to tell me I just had an hallucination? That those Nikki Sixx guitar picks are so common around here that Tommy could easily have one of his own? Of course, that wouldn't explain what happened to Danica's, which has mysteriously disappeared, according to her younger sister Darlene."

Keith's adam's apple bobbed down and up as he swallowed with exaggerated noise. "Yowza. Well, uh, then I guess we should go find the sheriff."

Shaking her head, Jamie turned to open her car door. "It's too late for that now; Tommy caught me looking at it." An abrupt, bitter laugh escaped her throat as she climbed into the driver's seat. "He had the gall to accuse me of putting it there to make him look guilty." She sighed heavily. "Well, *adiós,* Keith. And thanks but no thanks for the watchdog service, if that's really what it was. I think I'll just go home and pack a suitcase, head for someplace far, far away, New

Zealand maybe. They probably have Dairy Queens, don't you suppose?"

Keith moved up to block the door from being closed. "What do you mean, 'if that's really what it was'? You think I was spying on you?"

"Well, you did act like a total jerk at the Dairy Queen today, just because I was there with Morey."

"Yeah, well, you told me you weren't interested in him."

"Yeah, well, maybe I changed my mind."

Frowning, Keith got out of the way so she could close the door. "Maybe I couldn't care less. Send me a postcard from New Zealand."

Jamie reached for the interior door handle and gave him a nasty smile. "Maybe I will!" she retorted, and slammed the door closed before Keith could get in the last word. Sometimes he was just sooo immature.

Driving home she thought about packing a suitcase when she got there, and it really didn't seem like a bad idea. The only problem was, she had less than five dollars to her name. That would hardly get her to Elk City, much less another country. And she supposed her father would get pretty suspicious if she requested several hundred dollars for gas. Then she remembered the blue-ribbon bonds being kept for her in a safety deposit box at the bank. Jamie knew where her father had hidden the key, but had never been tempted to use it. For one thing, as president of the bank her father had at least a dozen pairs of eyes in the place, and one of them would surely catch her in the act. Also, money from the sale of those bonds was strictly for her college education. But she would have to strenuously avoid college if it was her fate to be a Dairy Princess. So why let the bonds just sit in that box and molder when they could be put to good use, such as saving her neck from Tommy Davidson's merciless hands?

When she turned onto her U-shaped street, she noted with relief that the house was still dark, a good sign that her parents hadn't arrived ahead of her. The driveway was empty, but that didn't mean anything, since they always parked their cars in the garage. Of utmost importance was the time, and the clock on Jamie's dash announced that it was just a few minutes after ten. No sweat. She doused her headlights and pulled into her usual spot, a narrow extension of concrete on the left side of the driveway, parked, and cut the engine. In her mind, she was already deciding what to pack and what to leave behind, quickly coming to the conclusion that one suitcase wasn't going to cut it. She'd probably need five or six, if she could find that many.

Thinking so seriously about running away, she started feeling a little sick. Her stomach was tied into knots by the time she got through the front door. It was a really scary thing to contemplate at her tender young age, but not nearly as scary as death, and she didn't know what else to do. She would never in a million years be able to convince

Sheriff Hammond that Tommy had killed Danica, even if she had the guitar pick. Tommy would claim she had planted it there, and naturally the sheriff would choose to believe him.

Closing the door behind her, she turned to find a small welcoming committee in the foyer. There wasn't much light, only what the coach lamp in the yard provided through the front door window's sheer curtains, but it was enough for her to recognize her parents and to see that they were not wearing smiles.

"I can explain—"

"Save your breath," her father cut in angrily. "I can smell you from here. Emergency keg party, right?"

Jamie's first thought was that he'd had too much to drink tonight, and had fallen and bumped his head. She didn't even like beer, thought it tasted totally gross. Then she remembered the gag toilet in Tommy's room. She had, in fact, been generously sprayed with Eau de Budweiser. And she could just see her parents buying that one. No sense in even trying.

"I did not go to a party. Listen to me, please, this is important. When we went to see Danica before the funeral—"

"You found a bruise on her neck that you thought looked like a handprint, which gave you the idea she'd been murdered. And since Tommy Davidson had threatened to strangle her, you assumed him responsible. You then confronted him, and he warned you that accusations of that

135

nature could be very hazardous to your health. How am I doing so far?"

The grapevine was operating with its usual efficient inefficiency. It was like a lump of modeling clay being passed around, each person making his or her own impression. God only knew what you'd have at the end of the line. An Agatha Christie novel, probably.

Jamie sighed. "The bruise was not in the shape of a handprint. It was just a small oval bruise behind her right ear that looked like it could have been made by thumb pressure." Jamie couldn't believe this. They were discussing Danica's death as if it were a movie they had just seen. "And Tommy did not threaten to strangle her, just kill." *Just* kill? God, it was getting worse. "As for the confronting-him part, that's what I just got back from doing, so you couldn't possibly have heard about that yet. He didn't say anything about my health. I think he was going to . . . well, I'll skip over that part. The pick! Yeah, Danica's Mötley Crüe guitar pick. It's really cool, red with Nikki Sixx's name embossed in gold on the back, and when I saw it there at Tommy's he tried to kill me!"

Apparently Hamilton Fox found that all very uninteresting. He leaned against the banister with a low grunt, his fingers steepled, a contemplative look on his face. "All right, listen up, young lady. This charade ends tonight. You are not Nancy Drew. These are very damaging rumors and this is the real world. Wake up to it! You will begin by handing over any extra keys to your car. I will take you to school in the mornings and your mother will pick you up. I'm adding another two weeks to your house arrest, and if you so much as step a hair out of line before the end of that period, you can kiss your personal telephone good-bye forever. You will not breathe another word of scandal. Whatever you do reflects on me, you know, and I think you've embarrassed me — this family — quite enough. Now go to your room, and not another word."

Jamie handed over the keys and slumped silently up the staircase.

Chapter Seven

The tantalizing aroma of bacon cooking rose up to greet Jamie as she descended the staircase the next morning. It activated her salivary glands, but it didn't lift her out of the dumps. She was down there deep, and she looked the way she felt. She hadn't bothered to put on makeup, and had barely run a brush through her hair, which almost looked like dreadlocks from all the tossing she'd done on her pillow last night. She wore an old sweater that sagged unevenly at the hem and was pilled and her most ragged pair of jeans.

Her parents were talking in hushed tones in the kitchen. Talking about her, probably, what a problem child she was. Maybe they should send her off to that survivalist wilderness thing, maybe that would coax some sense into her. Where had they gone wrong? Was she not of the same genes that produced her sensible, normal brother?

Jamie thought about eavesdropping, but she was too low to really care what was being said about her. She dragged herself on into the kitchen, and as she'd anticipated, her parents' voices fell silent the moment she appeared. Gloria was suddenly very busy at the stove, and her father buried his nose deeper into the financial section of the morning paper as he reached for his steaming coffee. Jamie cleared her throat. Not to get their attention, but she knew that's what they'd think.

Gloria turned, feigning surprise. "Good mor — Good grief, Jamie, you're not going to school looking like that, are you?"

Jamie's father glanced in their direction over the top of the paper, his eyes registering clear disapproval before returning to the task of reading. Jamie was a little surprised he hadn't ordered her to march right back upstairs and put on some decent clothes and do something with the witch's broom on her head. Maybe he felt bad about ruining her whole life.

"Mom, most of my peers look this bad every day."

"Well, that doesn't mean you have to. What do you want for breakfast?"

Shuffling over to the table, Jamie shrugged. "I don't care. Whatever." She was reaching for the front section of the paper when her mother stepped up behind her and gently grabbed her forearm. Jamie looked back at her, confused.

"What's going on?"

A sudden look of distress came over her mother's face. She pulled her eyes away from Jamie's and gazed down at the newspaper.

Pressed her lips together with a slight quiver in her chin. And Jamie felt her heart drop a few inches. Something bad had happened. There had been another death. Someone close to her, one of the guys. Keith—Oh, Lord, what if Tommy had—or Keith might have—

Oh God Oh God Oh God, don't let it be!

"Who was it, Mom? Was it Keith?" Jamie's voice came out as a dry croak. Images rushed through her head, horrible, unbearable images. If she'd already eaten her breakfast, she was sure she'd be blowing it.

"Honey, it's Alan. They've got him up at the hospital in Elk City, listed in critical condition. He . . . he tried to commit suicide last night."

A wave of subdued relief clashed with a wave of cold fear. Very slowly, Jamie pulled out the captain's chair nearest her and lowered herself into it, her face bleached white. It was possible, she supposed. Maybe he'd watched his parents go at each other's throats just one too many times. Maybe he looked into the future and saw himself hopelessly trapped inside a bottle, nowhere to go but down the drain.

But maybe he'd had a little visit from Tommy. The same Tommy whose nose he'd bashed with an empty liquor bottle last Saturday night. But who would believe it? Not only was Alan an alcoholic with a miserable home life, he had also signed the blood pact. But Alan was still alive. If he pulled through, and surely he would, he could set the record straight.

140

After giving Jamie a consoling pat on the shoulder, her mother quietly went back to her cooking. Her father continued to hide behind the financial section. Jamie reluctantly unfolded the paper to the front page, where she expected the story about Alan to be, thinking what a field day the *Deer Creek Review* was having. There hadn't been this much juicy local news in years, not since the pastor of the Presbyterian church ran off with his secretary and her husband had gone berserk, shooting out a bunch of shop windows downtown.

She was right; the story was on the front page, top left. Under the caption SECOND SUICIDE ATTEMPTED was a picture of Alan, the one from last year's school yearbook. He looked drunk, and probably had been, sitting there wearing an Alfred E. Newman smile. What, me worry? Jamie sighed and lowered her watery gaze to read the column beneath. *Just don't die, Alan, please. You've got at least one good reason to live. We love to watch you fall down.*

According to the sheriff's department, at approximately half past ten last night, Mrs. Edna Quinn had been taking the garbage out when she noticed exhaust smoke pouring from underneath the doors of the large shed behind the garage in which her son Alan, a senior at Heritage Academy, typically parked his white 1983 Chevrolet pickup. Mrs. Quinn reported that she also heard the rumbling of an engine, and at once became alarmed. When she ran to open the shed's doors,

141

a considerable cloud of exhaust escaped into the night air. She found Alan inside the truck, slumped unconscious behind the steering wheel. He had been rushed to the Elk City hospital where doctors listed him in critical condition. Sheriff Hammond confirmed that Alan Quinn was also a participant in the suicide pact delivered to the mayor's office, but was quick to add that Alan was known to have a drinking problem which might as easily have been accountable for his actions. When Mayor Shepherd was contacted for his comment on the situation, he offered nothing but condolences for the Quinn family and friends of Alan Quinn. He said that he and his own family "would remember them in prayer."

Jamie felt numb. This was all so unreal. Danica, now Alan. It had been just before ten when she'd left Tommy, him madder than a wet hornet and trembling with the strength of a bull. A forest fire of rage, no way to put it out but satisfy it, let it spend itself on whatever might be available. Like Alan Quinn—though Tommy had probably planned to get him anyway, sooner or later. Who next? Herself? Oh yes, she could bank on it. And the sheriff would be quoted as saying, "Yes, Jamie Fox was one of the knuckleheads, but let me add that she was known to be a troubled teenager. Always getting grounded or losing her car. She was also under a lot of pressure from her father to make something spectacular of herself. She had her reasons for wanting to stick her head in the microwave oven."

Would Tommy stop then, or would he recognize the opportunity for two more freebies, Keith and Roman, the last living cosigners of the blood pact who also had obvious reasons for wanting to cash in their chips. Maybe by this time Tommy would have developed a healthy bloodlust, and would never be able to stop until someone else stopped him, most probably with a 12-gauge shotgun.

She shuddered, going on to the adjacent article under the headline SURVEY REVEALS MAYOR DECLINE.

Lorna Baker, a *Review* staff writer, had written an article based on a telephone survey among local residents. It seemed that Eugene Shepherd's long-lived career as mayor of Deer Creek might be slipping away from him. Nearly sixty-five percent of those questioned were of the opinion that demolition of the old railroad depot should have been halted until the suicide threat had been confronted and eliminated by all possible means. One resident, who wished to remain anonymous, had been quoted as saying, "He just acted like those kids' lives meant nothing at all to him. And what's that old building worth? Not two cents, if you ask me. Shepherd was the one who came up with that statue idea, I don't think anybody else in this town was turning cartwheels over it. Seems to me he's lost sight of what's really important, so my vote's going to Malcolm Monroe."

Smiling, Malcolm Monroe let the paper drop to

the table and shot a fist into the air as a gesture of victory. "Yes! You're looking at the new mayor of Deer Creek. Next stop—Governor of Oklahoma! Honey, break out the champagne. We've got cause to celebrate!"

His wife gave him a disapproving look. "Good heavens, Malcolm, it's only seven-thirty in the morning."

Morey swallowed his mouthful of pancakes. "So?"

Barbara Monroe shook her perfectly coiffed head, her dark eyes rolled up to the ceiling. "So we're not going to have champagne. Besides, I wouldn't call this a time to celebrate. That poor boy. Wait until the election returns are in, Malcolm. We'll have our champagne then."

For a few minutes they ate their breakfasts in silence, Morey reading the comic page, his father rereading the article about Shepherd's decline in popularity, both wearing the same half-smile. Barbara sipped at her coffee wondering whether or not she should bring up the rumor she'd heard at the beauty shop yesterday afternoon. She finally decided she should. Her husband needed to be informed of everything going on in Deer Creek.

"Malcolm," she said, tracing the rim of her cup with a red-taloned fingertip. "Have you heard anything about a Tommy Davidson?"

Morey looked up from the comic page, chewing very slowly.

Malcolm sat back in his chair. "I haven't had

much time for gossip lately. What about him?"

"Well," Barbara said as she carefully placed her cup back in its saucer, "when I went to the beauty shop yesterday afternoon, Ruth, you know, the girl who does my hair, told me that one of her earlier customers overheard a clerk at Gertrude's Fashions telling the cashier that Tommy might have been involved in that girl's death. I know it's hardly a subject to discuss over breakfast, but they said a bloody hammer had been found in her room."

Malcolm scowled. "Nobody in this town has anything better to do than wag their tongues. I do believe that if a hammer had been used on the girl, both the sheriff and the coroner would have noticed, don't you? They may be stupid but they're not blind. I don't like it, though. I want people to be thinking about what a dirty skunk Shepherd is. Next to a cold-blooded hammer fiend, even Gene Shepherd looks pretty good." He chewed his inner cheek thoughtfully for a few seconds, then turned to his son. "Morey, do you know anything about this?"

Morey's eyes darted to his mother's and back. He cleared his throat. "Why would I?"

Malcolm rubbed his chin thoughtfully. "Well, it's just a crazy rumor. It'll probably die down pretty soon."

Trudging up the tile steps to the school building's second floor where her classes were held, Jamie became aware of all the furtive whispering beneath the usual morning cacophony of laughter, shouts, and locker doors banging shut. Though she tried, she couldn't make out what was being said, but she knew they had to be talking about Alan's so-called attempted suicide. That and maybe trading stories they'd heard about Tommy Davidson.

There was a throng climbing the steps behind her, but Jamie suddenly had the feeling that someone back there was staring a hole in the back of her head. The urge to turn around and look was overwhelming, but Jamie, feeling self-conscious without her makeup, forced her eyes to remain focused straight ahead. Then a lead weight settled in the pit of her stomach as a dreadful suspicion arose with each step. It was probably Tommy. His intense hatred was aimed and projected at her like a laser beam, and if looks could kill, her head would probably explode right about now, raining brains and blood over all the kids in the stairwell.

When she reached the top, she hurriedly bullied her way to her locker, tempted to jump inside it and hide. Her hands were shaking so badly she flubbed twice on the combination. She didn't think Tommy would dare try anything at school, not in front of so many witnesses, but that didn't serve to calm her any. She didn't want to face that psychopath at all.

On her third try she finally got her locker opened, and was reaching for her American Literature text on the shelf when it became obvious that someone was standing right behind her. So close she could hear his breathing. Maybe Keith or Roman (please!) . . . or both of them . . . but why didn't they say anything? Was this a new game they'd invented, give Jamie a heart attack?

"Hello, Fox."

Jamie recognized the voice and felt a new kind of panic. It wasn't Keith's or Roman's—or Tommy Davidson's, thank God—it was Morey's voice. For the first time ever, he'd approached her in the hallway before class, hopefully to flirt. And here she was without a single bit of makeup on her face! What had she been thinking this morning?

Slowly she turned, blushing furiously, a sheepish smile on her unglossed lips. "Hi, Morey."

To her further embarrassment, he stepped back half a pace and cocked his head. "You look different today. What did you do?"

Jamie cleared her throat, feeling her cheeks burn hotter. "Actually it's what I didn't do. I was so depressed this morning I didn't bother to put on any makeup, or fix my hair. I look really gross, huh?"

He made a great show of mentally debating the issue, which embarrassed Jamie even more, but it also made her mad. Some days he looked a little less than perfect, but she'd never think of telling him so, even if he asked.

Finally he ended the charade with a laugh. "I was just putting you on. Actually I think you're prettier without makeup."

His compliment was punctuated by the shrill sound of the first bell, which meant they had five minutes to get to their classrooms and their seats. Jamie silently cursed it.

Morey sighed. "Just another day in paradise. Well, I wanted to ask you if you'd like to take a drive with me tonight. Maybe go down to the old mill bridge and look at the stars."

Jamie thought that sounded suspiciously like an invitation to make out. She certainly hoped so. And it would be absurd to assume he would only want to kiss her for more information, which he could get by merely asking. He really did like her for herself. She could see them down at the old mill bridge counting stars — in each other's eyes. Then her mind made a quantum, ludicrous leap to her trying on extravagant wedding gowns in Marcelea's Boutique. It truly was a day in paradise.

Fool's paradise. Reality suddenly came down like a ton of bricks.

"God, I'd love to, but I can't, I'm still grounded. For a whole month now."

"So what? You can sneak out, can't you?"

Sure, she could sneak out. She could swallow a bottle of Liquid Plumber, too, which would be just about as wise. Jamie had a vision of herself with gray hair and pruney skin, hobbling precariously behind a cane to check the calendar and see how many days left until her freedom was restored and she got her car keys back. "Well, I guess, but my parents don't go to bed until ten-thirty. That's awful late, don't you think?"

Morey smiled and reached out to gently squeeze her shoulder. "We're young, we can take it. I'll pick you up at the nearest corner at ten-forty-five."

At noon the atmosphere in the cafeteria was boisterous as usual, sounding like a high trading spree at the New York Stock Exchange. Except for the table where Jamie, Keith, and Roman sat, painfully aware of their two missing comrades. It was almost twenty after and they hadn't still said a single word to each other, nor had any of them shown much interest in eating even though today's entree actually looked and smelled edible.

Jamie finally pushed her tray away with a sigh. Her head felt like a ping-pong ball after going back and forth so many times on the issue of sneaking out tonight. Part of her said, "Break a date with Morey Monroe? What, are you crazy?" The other part said, "Sneak out of your house when you're already up to your eyeballs in trouble? What, are you crazy?" And as if that wasn't enough to *make* her go crazy, there was Alan to worry about, and how to nail Tommy Davidson before he nailed the rest of them.

She put the issue with Morey on hold for a minute and looked over at Keith. "How long did you hang around Tommy's last night after I left?"

"About two seconds. You think I'm crazy or something?"

Why not join the club? Jamie thought dismally.

149

"I don't suppose you happened to see Tommy leave right after you did?"

Keith pushed his tray away with his elbows. "No. Not right after, anyway. I was sure checking it in my rearview mirror. Uh, speaking of Tommy, he's been giving me and Roman the evil eye all morning. Made me so nervous I flunked the geometry test."

Roman had scooped up a spoonful of mashed potatoes, and was obviously making calculations for catapulting it to the ceiling. "I know what you're thinking, Jamie. I agree. And I think he's going to go after me or Keith next." He shot the load of potatoes into the air with true aim, but the missile did not stick. It fell squarely onto the head of a junior named Amber Wesley, who shrieked and frantically brushed it out of her hair while her friends scanned the area for a snide, guilty grin. Roman, Jamie, and Keith wore identical stony poker faces which they had the ability to maintain for long periods of time, no matter how tempted they were to laugh, which eliminated them from suspicion as Amber looked their way. But today the look didn't take much effort.

Keith tiredly propped his chin in his upturned palms. "So what do you suggest we do, Roman, get to him first? Maybe arrange a little crossbow accident?"

"Get real, Keith," Jamie snapped. "Whatever we do, it has to be legal."

"You're such a nitpicker," Keith complained facetiously.

"Don't mean to change the subject," Roman said, "well, maybe I do, but did you hear about the massive kegger planned for Saturday night? At the old depot. The farewell party. Nobody can leave until they puke."

"And I have to miss it," Jamie groaned, thinking that Morey would be there. Alone. Gorgeous as always. Wanting to party. But not alone. How unfair life could be.

Keith suddenly straightened. "Uh-oh."

His ominous tone, combined with the genuine fear registered in his eyes, now focused above Jamie's left shoulder, made her want to scramble under the table for cover. This time it was not just paranoia. Tommy Davidson was right behind her. She thought for a moment she was going to faint.

He leaned over her, planting a huge hairy hand, knuckle-side down, on the table beside her. Jamie was afraid anything she said might set him off, so she kept her mouth closed and waited anxiously to see what he would do next. She expected him to pick up the faded aqua plate from her tray and mash the contents into her face. That would be just fine with her, as long as he didn't twist her head off afterward.

"You wanting to start something, Tommy?" Keith asked in the politest tone possible. Nevertheless Jamie kicked him under the table, glaring. If he was trying to impress her with his bravery, let him do it on his side of the table.

Tommy chuckled deep in his throat. "Not me,

no. I never start anything, Maguire, but most of the time I do end up finishing it. I just came over to tell y'all how truly sorry I am about your buddy Alan. Oh, and to give Jamie here something she left over at my house last night." Jamie watched Tommy's hand disappear, then reappear a few seconds later with Danica's Nikki Sixx guitar pick. He stuck it in her untouched ball of mashed potatoes and said, "I should have kept it, but I'm just too honest." Issuing a sinister laugh, he swaggered away from their table.

Jamie stared blankly at the pick, thankful he hadn't made her swallow it. His returning it took her completely by surprise, but it really shouldn't have. If she'd been thinking a little less about her planned illicit rendezvous with Morey and more about the situation with Tommy, she probably would have expected it, even predicted it. If she really had tried to plant the pick on him as evidence, certainly he would return it. Keeping it would make that claim look a little flimsy, make him look a little guilty. She knew it must have twirked him royally to give it up, but he was smart enough to realize he just couldn't afford to keep it. That was the most surprising thing, seeing evidence that Tommy actually had half a brain.

His expression grim as a hearse driver's, Roman reached over and gingerly withdrew the pick from Jamie's mashed potatoes. "Danica's Nikki Sixx pick. Why did you take it over to Tommy's?"

Jamie handed him her napkin to clean the potato off. "I didn't, that's just his defense. I saw it pinned under a thumbtack on one of his Mötley Crüe posters. Which proves that he killed Danica. But it won't convince the sheriff. Tommy'll just say I planted it over there to get him busted, and today, being the honest guy he is, he gave it back. Get the picture?"

"Wouldn't his parents know if he took off after ten last night?" Keith asked, looking at Jamie with wide, hopeful eyes.

She shook her head. "His dad thought he was there when he wasn't. Forget that."

The bell rang, signaling the end of the second-ary-level lunch period. Jamie, Keith, and Roman rose dejectedly to their feet, carrying their trays as if they weighed fifty pounds apiece. Jamie discreetly looked around for Morey, finding him holding up the far green wall with his left shoulder as he listened raptly to two of his giggling fans. One of them was apparently telling him a joke, because suddenly he threw his head back and released a hearty belly laugh. Jamie's nostrils flared as jealousy flooded through her. So much for the internal debate. She would sneak out to meet Morey tonight, and that was final. The odds couldn't be against her *all* the time.

Could they?

Chapter Eight

Looking at the clock on her nightstand late that evening, Jamie sighed heavily. Time seemed to be dragging by so slowly she was beginning to suspect she'd entered some sort of warp zone. She thought it might help if she'd stop checking the clock every fifteen seconds, but she couldn't stop herself. She was so nervous she could hardly keep herself from climbing the walls.

To get her mind off the amount of time she still had to wait (forty-one minutes and sixteen — no, fifteen — seconds) she wondered how Roman and Keith's little venture was going. Keith had called shortly after Jamie and her parents had finished eating dinner to tell her of his and Roman's plan to snoop around Alan's place to see if any evidence linking Tommy to the scene could be found. Roman had even gotten his mother to make them a gallon of plaster of paris for making molds of tire prints. Talk about your basic set of Keystone Kops. Picturing those two out there in trenchcoats, deerhunter caps, and fake beards pouring plaster of paris into every depression in sight gave Jamie a case of the giggles, and once they got started, she couldn't turn them off. Her frayed nerves were apparently making her hysterical. Afraid that her parents might hear her and think she was up in her room sniffing hair spray or something, she finally resorted to recalling the image of Danica hanging purple-faced in her bedroom. The giggle-well instantly went dry.

"Oh, Danica." Jamie curled up on her bed with her pillow, summoning earlier, pleasant memories, starting with the day they'd first met. At first, they hadn't liked each other at all. Danica had thought Jamie was stuck-up because her father was the bank president and they lived in the nicer part of town. Jamie had thought Danica was a dopehead. Wrong. Just a dope.

The goofy greeting cards they used to make each other . . .

The ridiculous spats they'd have over who'd gotten the biggest slice of cake . . .

The poor little bunny rabbit that got stuck in the plaster of paris . . .

Jamie had fallen asleep unaware, drifting smoothly into a strange dream about hapless rabbits becoming embedded in plaster of paris, which for some reason was all over the ground in separate pools, like miniature quicksand traps. Looking around, she saw that some people had gotten one or both of their feet stuck in them, too. The ones with both feet captured were having a terrible time keeping their balance, reminding her of flagpoles in a high wind.

Following some inexplicable trail of logic, she soon found herself trapped in a rough-hewn stone dungeon containing a vast number of safety deposit boxes. She had committed some heinous crime—she couldn't remember exactly what it was, only that it was heinous—and as punishment, she was going to be shot with a crossbow by a black-hooded man who looked suspiciously like her father. It was time, and she could hear him coming. He was rattling his keys, her car keys, probably just to torment her because she'd made the *Guinness Book of World Records* by getting the all-time-lowest scores on the SAT.

At the fateful instant the arrow was released, Jamie bolted upright with a silent scream on her lips, heart thundering. Her widened eyes darted to the clock and she gasped loudly. It was ten to eleven! She was already five minutes late!

Scrambling off the bed, she rushed to the window and peered into the murky darkness, but trees obstructed her view of the nearest corner. She couldn't tell if Morey was still waiting or not. She could only hope as she quickly straightened her clothes, brushed her hair, applied more cherry gloss to her lips and another few dabs of White Linen, her best perfume, behind her ears and in the hollow at the base of her throat. She could kick herself for falling asleep like that. But maybe Morey had decided to give her an extra ten or fifteen minutes, allowing for unforeseen delays that might have been caused by her parents. Then again, he might have glanced at his Rolex at ten-forty-six and written her off on the spot. He was Morey Monroe; he didn't have to put up with this. If Jamie thought she could keep him waiting, she had another think coming.

Jamie held her breath as she carefully pulled her bedroom door open about a foot, then stuck her head out to reconnoiter the hallway. Both it and the downstairs area were silent and dark. A little too silent, actually. It made her wonder if her parents were crouched hidden somewhere in the dark, waiting to spring their trap. "Aha! We knew you'd try to sneak out!"

Jamie pushed the paranoid thought from her mind. Her parents had a little more savvy than that. They did, for sure. Still, Jamie felt as if she were walking through enemy territory as she left her bedroom and crept down the staircase, nearly jumping out of her skin at every little sound. The dark shapes of the living-room furniture had never seemed so ominous before. The sofa was Early American with a high back; it was easy to imagine her parents sitting in it right now, completely concealed by the gloom, both wearing in-frared goggles. Who knew, maybe it was the latest sex thrill.

But much to her relief no one called out to ask why she was creeping through the house like a cat burglar. She made it outside with the barest minimum of noise, a miracle considering her degree of nervousness. Normally when Jamie was extremely nervous, she was as also clumsy as a hippo on a highwire.

After silently closing the back door to the utility room, she started running. By now she had to be at least ten minutes late, moving on to fifteen. She just knew Morey's car wouldn't be there and then she definitely *would* kick herself, all the way to Tulsa and back.

But the Ferrari was there. Jamie saw it and came to a sudden halt, holding a hand over her heart to keep it from jumping out. Hard as she was breathing, one would think she'd run five miles instead of just half a block. Morey was out of the car, leaning against the hood with his arms crossed.

Here we go, Jamie thought as she continued toward him, keeping her eyes on the ground. She had an urge to look back and see if any of the front curtains in her house were pulled aside—maybe she could spot a pair of binoculars—but she resisted it. If the dungeon was her destiny, she'd rather find out when she could tell herself that it had all been worth it.

When she was within speaking distance Morey said, "I was about to give up on you. In about three more minutes, I'd have been gone."

"Sorry, I, uh, sort of fell asleep," Jamie muttered as she followed him to the passenger side of his car. He opened the door for her and she slid in, aware of an all-over tingling sensation. How jealous his gushing little groupies would be if they could see her now.

Morey hopped in the driver's seat and started

the Ferrari's quiet engine, then turned on the radio before pulling away from the curb. The song playing was "High Enough" by Damn Yankees, one of Jamie's favorites. She hummed along with the chorus and had no doubt whatsoever that Morey could take her all the way to the golden streets of heaven.

He waited until they were a few blocks away before turning on the headlights. "So, what's the latest?"

Jamie shrugged. "Same old crap, I guess."

Morey reached over and switched off the radio. "I mean about Tommy Davidson. Did you get any proof yet?"

Jamie was hardly in the mood to talk about Tommy Davidson. She'd taken a giant risk sneaking out tonight, and she wanted to have fun, feel good, experience an excellent adventure of her own, something that would make her diary blush. "No. Unfortunately. Hey, you mind if I turn the radio back on? I like that Damn Yankee song."

Seemingly somewhat irritated by her request, Morey turned it back on for her, but the song had already changed. He left it on at low volume. "Well, like what exactly have you done? Have you gone over to his house or nosed around in his car?"

"If you don't mind, I'd really rather not talk about Tommy," Jamie said apologetically. "Just thinking about him is going to put me in a bad mood."

Morey obviously did want to talk about

Tommy, but for the time being he let the subject drop and started telling her about his new computer game, some sort of complex story maze. Before Jamie knew it, they were coming up on the old mill bridge. Morey slowed the car to a crawl as the front tires bumped over the thick wooden planks. Above them, Spanish moss and a tangled network of naked vines dangled from the rusted iron braces. In the sparse moonlight, Jamie decided the bridge was far more spooky than romantic.

In the middle of the one-way bridge, Morey brought the car to a stop and doused the headlights, then put the transmission in park and cut the engine. Without the engine running they could hear the quiet gurgling of the Canadian river beneath them. Jamie remembered the last time, a few years ago, that the gang had packed picnic lunches and come out here to fish for bass from this bridge. On the south bank Keith had found a thick vine attached to a large oak tree, and yelling like Tarzan had attempted to swing to the other side. But the vine had broken, and so had Keith's arm when he'd hit the ground.

"Let's get out," Morey said, opening his door.

Jamie's pulse quickened. "Okay."

The wind by the river seemed much cooler, and joining Morey in front of the car Jamie shivered inside her blue-and-white-striped cardigan sweater. "Feels like winter's on the way," she said, hoping he would get the hint and put his arms around her.

He did not disappoint. Drawing her close to him, he enveloped her with the sides of his windbreaker like a pair of wings. The windbreaker's lining was warm and cozy and smelled faintly of Downy fabric softener. She could feel Morey's heart beating fast, betraying his excitement. Jamie knew this was the right moment to lift her face and receive the kiss he was waiting to give. So why didn't she do it?

"I've been thinking," he began.

Jamie closed her eyes. *Yes? Yes? About the prom . . . ? Asking me to go steady?* The long moment of suspense was excruciating.

"Tommy Davidson strikes me as being a total loser. If he did what you said, murdered Danica and made it look like suicide, I wouldn't put it past him to steal something while he was at it. Know what I mean?"

In spite of the toasty embrace, Jamie shivered again. She didn't understand why Morey's words should cause such an inner chill, but they had, and it wouldn't go away. She started to tell him about the guitar pick she'd found in Tommy's private living quarters, but changed her mind and obeyed an intuitive impulse to play dumb instead. "Not really. If he'd stolen anything, I'm sure her parents would have noticed."

"Maybe, maybe not. Remember the saying 'Out of sight, out of mind'? Besides, he probably wouldn't have taken anything real obvious, like the TV or stereo. The thing is, if you can find something of hers in his stuff, there's your proof.

If you want, I'll go with you to look. We can cut out during lunch tomorrow and do it then."

Jamie was all but drowning in a whirlpool of conflicting thoughts. There was nothing suspicious about his reasoning; it was a close echo of her own, except that she'd known exactly what she was looking for at Tommy's. But there was an undertone of insistence in Morey's voice that seemed a little out of place, considering that he'd hardly known Danica. Maybe he was thinking it would help his dad's political career if he was instrumental in bringing a killer to justice. Which would mean he was just using her. Again. But that didn't make much sense, letting her get half the credit. He should want it all. So what the hell was going on?

"I don't know, Morey, I'll sleep on it." She lifted her face for the magic kiss she'd so far only dreamed of and read about in romance novels, only to find that Morey was glaring down at her.

"Don't you care about your friend? Don't you want Tommy to get what he deserves?"

Jamie suddenly pushed herself out of his embrace, matching his glare. "You bet I do. More than you'll ever know. What I can't figure out is where you're coming from. Why should you care, Morey? Why is this so important to you? Because I get the feeling that it is, very important, and it has nothing to do with Danica or Tommy. Are you doing this for your dad's campaign? I thought he already had this election in the bag."

His lips compressed in a thin line, jaw muscles

162

bulging, Morey lifted his set of keys from one of the pockets in his windbreaker and began searching for the ignition key in a spill of moonlight. "I was only trying to help. You don't have to turn into such a megabitch."

Jamie bristled at the insulting name. Megabitch, eh? Well, if that's what he wanted. "Give me a break. Guys like you don't help for squat unless there's something in it for you. Or in your case, for your old man."

Locating the correct key, he turned and stiffly skirted the front bumper to open the driver's door. Before ducking in he growled, "Keep it up, you'll be walking back home."

Jamie estimated that the distance from here to there was about four miles, and most of that was lonely country road. She didn't savor the idea of walking it alone in the dead of night. But at the moment, she'd rather walk across fifty miles of burning desert sand than spend another ten minutes with Morey in his ego cruiser. What a jerk he was to even threaten such a thing. No wonder he didn't have a steady girlfriend.

"What's the matter, can't take the truth?" she shouted, bending over to meet his new eye level through the open passenger window. "Try this on for size. I think I just figured out why you're so motivated to help your dad get to the White House. Because you've got the same ambition, don't you? You're not your father's son, you're his clone! And all you do is use people; to you, they're just rungs on the ladder. And God help the person who tries to stand in your way. Right? Am I right?"

Morey said nothing, nor did he look at her. Staring straight ahead, he turned the key in the ignition and started his car's engine, revving it menacingly several times. Jamie was suddenly struck by a pang of paranoia that he might try to run her down. She should've quit while she was still ahead, but no, that was apparently a lesson she was never going to learn. Morey turned on his headlights, and she quickly straightened, her legs on red alert. If she could just make it safely off the bridge, there was plenty of woods around to hide in.

But Morey didn't try to go after her with his car. He very calmly put the stick in reverse and slowly began backing away, blinding her with his headlights. She averted her gaze from the unbearable brightness, restraining the urge to scrounge the ground for rocks to throw at his precious Italian sports car. How absolutely humiliating. This was going to make her diary blush, all right, with utter shame. She had to be the biggest fool on earth.

She waited until the beams of Morey's headlights had completely disappeared down the bisecting old mill road before she started walking. She wished she'd or worn her buckskin jacket, but she'd counted on Morey keeping her warm. Hah! That was the laugh of the century. She'd just have to suffer, and she deserved it. Huddled down in her sweater, she shuffled along the dirt road like an old bag lady who'd long since lost her dignity. A few minutes later, the nearby hoot of an owl brought her heart up to her throat and temporarily put a tiger in the bag lady's tank, speeding Jamie up considerably for several dozen yards until the panic passed and she slowed down to her previous dejected shuffle.

She tried not to think about Morey, how he had made a fool of her, by concentrating on her disquieting surroundings. Things slithered stealthily in the tall grass. Swaying branches spoke of unseen eyes watching her from the treetops. Now and then she heard the distant whinny of a horse or lowering of a cow. Ghostly wisps of clouds kept blocking the moonlight, casting her into deeper darkness.

But no matter how hard she tried, Morey kept popping up in her thoughts. At least she'd shown some spunk, told him off. And he knew she'd spoken the truth. At least one person in Deer Creek had his number, had seen his true colors. His father might not have, but Morey probably had done some backflips over the newspaper article on Danica's death. In fact, if she didn't know better, she'd suspect that Morey himself killed Danica, hoping for just the effect her "suicide" had had on the community.

Eyes wide, Jamie came to a sudden stop. She *did* know better. Morey couldn't possibly be that ruthless. But then she remembered him leaving the cafeteria on Monday, the day Danica died, announcing that he was going to Dairy Queen for some decent food. Was that really where he'd gone? Was Tommy truly stupid enough to kill Danica only two days after he had publicly threatened to do so?

Was she having these thoughts only because she was mad at Morey and subconsciously wanted revenge, or had she just unwittingly stumbled onto a blacker truth? With no knowledge of the missing guitar pick, Morey's idea about possibly finding something of Danica's among Tommy's possessions was tentative at best. So why was he so damn insistent about it? That more than anything made Jamie sick with dread.

Seldom was Jamie in the right place at the right time, and tonight was no exception. It was probably getting close to eleven-thirty, far too late to be calling on people. But she was coming up on the right place, the old farmstead where Nancy Leibelle lived, and Jamie felt a desperate need to know if Morey had gone to the Dairy Queen for lunch on Monday like he'd said.

Loose gravel crunched loudly under her shoes as she walked up the narrow drive leading to Nancy Leibelle's white clapboard farmhouse. There were no lights on inside the two-story structure, and its dark, towering silhouette was quite intimidating, almost sinister-looking at that time of night, but determination pressed Jamie onward until she heard a low growl coming from the front porch. Then she froze instantly, torn between pretending to be a statue and turning to run for her life. The unseen dog — a gigantic pit bull, in Jamie's imagination—growled a little louder, adding a couple of very unfriendly barks to his frightening repertoire.

Maybe the odds *were* always against her.

She couldn't decide what to do, not knowing if the dog was chained or loose. And she really didn't feel like trying to outrun a vicious pit bull. Now would be a good time for her fairy godmother to step in. Or Superman or Robocop or the Teenage Mutant Ninja Turtles. Anybody.

Then, like a beacon of mercy, the porch light came on and the front door creaked open. Nancy Leibelle stepped out in her robe and slippers, softly asking the dog what in tarnation he was barking at, as if he could tell her. Jamie could see Nancy peering in her direction and decided she'd better speak before Nancy became alarmed and went for the shotgun.

"Mrs. Leibelle! It's me, Jamie Fox!"

The dog, which Jamie could now see was just a border collie, continued to growl menacingly.

"Shut up, Blackie," Nancy snapped, giving him a gentle whap on the head that silenced him for about five seconds. "Land sakes, girl, what are you doing out here this time of night? Your car break down? Come on up here to the porch, Blackie won't bite."

Jamie reluctantly moved forward. "I'm really sorry about this. Guess I got you out of bed."

"Good guess," Nancy agreed, but her tone carried no hint of anger. "Now it's my turn. I bet you're in sore need of a telephone. Well, it's in

167

the kitchen, just follow me."

Jamie hung back at the bottom of the steps, not much liking the way Blackie was looking at her. "Actually, I don't need to use your phone. I just . . . I wanted to ask you a question. It's something I really need to know. Last Monday—did any teenagers come in for lunch that day?"

Nancy turned and gave her a funny look. "You came out here practically in the middle of the night to ask me that?"

"Well, I was already in the neighborhood," Jamie mumbled, hoping fervently that Nancy didn't tell anyone about her little visit.

Placing a hand on her hip, Nancy shook her head slowly. "You kids. I just thank the good Lord mine are all grown, or I'd probably be having strokes." Then an intensely reflective look came over her face as she worked on remembering last Monday. "There was a few little ones in with their mothers, you know, preschool kids. Mostly it was the same secretary crowd. Don't see any teenagers except for on the weekends. Isn't there a rule saying you can't leave the school property during lunchtime?"

Jamie nodded, her expression clearly showing just how she felt about that particular rule. "Yes, but like every other rule, it occasionally gets broken by a renegade. Like last Monday. A senior left the school property at noon saying he was going to eat at the Dairy Queen. So are you saying that he definitely wasn't there? I have to know for sure."

Jamie could almost read the weathered older woman's mind. She was thinking that there had to be a pretty interesting little story behind this question, and it was obvious she was dying to hear it. Jamie decided on the spot that if Nancy succumbed to her gossipy instincts and asked for an explanation, what she would get was *Zip. Nada.* Nothing. Let her make up her own. People in Deer Creek were very good at that anyway.

"I had to go to the bathroom a couple of times during the lunch hour," Nancy answered carefully, her gaze focused keenly on the black horizon. "Got this terrible bladder infection, you know. Second one in eight weeks. But I couldn't have been in there more than a couple of minutes, and nobody gets in and out that fast. Not at noon, anyway. If he was there, I'd have seen him, and I'm sure I would've remembered. You always remember the unusual. Now what's this all about, if you don't mind me askin'. You've got my curiosity up."

For a few seconds Jamie just looked at her. One sentence had stuck in her mind and kept repeating over and over like a phonograph needle snagged on a scratched LP. If he was there, I'd have seen him, and I'm sure I would've remembered. *If he was there, I'd have seen him.*

I'd have seen him.

Gooseflesh crawled up Jamie's arms and around her shoulders. But that was no kind of evidence. Certainly not proof. Maybe he changed his mind and went home for lunch. Or to the cafe. Or to the drugstore for a Coke and candy bar and afterward driving around, enjoying his illicit freedom.

But what if . . . ?

"Jamie, are you okay?"

Jamie snapped out of her unpleasant reverie and shivered as a gust of cold wind whipped around her. "Yeah, sure, I'm fine, fine. I just don't think . . . I mean, you deserve to know why you're losing sleep, but I can't really talk about it right now. Hope you understand. Well, thank you very, very much, and I'm so sorry about getting you out of bed, and I promise it'll never happen again. Anyway, I guess I'll be going now. 'Bye." She turned and started walking away before Nancy could attempt to pry the story out of her.

"Would you like to borrow a jacket?" Nancy called after her. "There's quite a chill in the air, feels like. You'll come down with a nasty cold."

The jacket sounded good, but next time she might not get away so easily. People around these parts had curiosity with muscle. "No thanks! I'll be fine!" she called back with a wave. She sounded convincing, at least to herself, but she felt anything but fine. A scene from the movie *Evil Dead II* came to mind, when the main character kept repeating to his reflection in a mirror that he was fine, he was fine, then suddenly his reflection jumped out of the mirror, grabbed him by the shoulders and softly said, *"Fine?* We just cut up our girlfriend with a chain saw. Does that sound *f-i-i-i-ne?"*

Jamie could relate. Here she was out in the sticks late at night, all alone except for the coyotes and snakes, freezing her butt off. If it hadn't been so late, she would have risked going into Nancy's house and using her phone to call Keith for a ride. But Keith's parents always went to bed around eight-thirty or nine, since their days started a good hour before the rooster crowed at dawn. They did not appreciate being wakened by the telephone.

She would have walked there, because she desperately needed to talk to Keith anyway, but the Maguires' dairy farm was twice the distance it was to town. Hugging herself against the cold, occasionally sniffling or coughing, apparently her body was not going to make a liar out of Nancy, she trudged along the lonely stretch of country road and tried not to think too much. It only gave her a headache.

Chapter Nine

She hadn't made a conscious decision to go by Roman's house before she went home, but she wasn't surprised to find herself turning down his street. She would ask him what she'd wanted to ask Keith—how their amateur detective operation tonight at Alan's had gone. A spine-tingling scenario flashed across the screen of her mind, Roman telling her in a conspiratorial whisper that they'd found some suspicious tire tracks near the Quinns' shed. They had made a plaster-of-paris impression of them, then took the hardened mold over to Tommy's for comparison with his Camaro's tires, finding that the tread was completely different. However, acting on a hunch, they'd snuck over to Morey's and compared the mold with his Ferrari's tires, and—hold on to your hat—

A perfect match. Morey's the one.

Jamie irritably swatted the image away as she would a fly. Her imagination was really working overtime. Until she had at least one solid, irrefutable piece of evidence pointing to Morey, she would grant him the benefit of the doubt. Even if he was a major-league jerk. No ifs, ands, or buts.

Roman's bedroom was in back of the house. Jamie had to let herself through the side gate of the stockyard fence which was next to the garage, then walk back to the other side of the house through dewy grass. It didn't take long for her turquoise and white Jordache running shoes to become uncomfortably damp. She sneezed stepping up to Roman's window, and the sound set off a neighbor's dog, and like a chain reaction, another dog joined in, and another and another, until it seemed that every dog within a fifty-mile radius was barking.

Gritting her teeth, Jamie tapped softly on Roman's dark bedroom window, wondering what time it was now. Way past midnight, surely. Maybe two or three in the morning. She tapped on the window again, more insistently. All those dogs barking were making her extremely nervous. If they kept it up, pretty soon the whole neighborhood would be awake, including Roman's parents.

Finally the curtains over Roman's window wavered, then parted. Without his glasses, he peered through the glass like a sleepy gopher.

"Roman, it's me, Jamie. Open the window," she hissed.

Roman blinked, obviously still half asleep. "Huh?"

Jamie made a lifting motion with her hands.

"Open the window! Come on, hurry up! I've gotta get out of here before lights start coming on."

It took the message a while to sink in, but finally Roman responded correctly and disconnected the latch. The window went up with a grating screech that made Jamie cringe. Why hadn't she just come with a marching band?

"What's going on?" Roman asked groggily, rubbing his eyes. "You know it's almost two in the morning?"

"I thought it was somewhere around two or three," Jamie said with a sniffle, followed by a slight cough. "Listen, I've got to know how things went at Alan's tonight. Did you find anything? Any suspicious tire tracks?"

Roman traded rubbing his eyes for stretching while he scratched his head. "Nah, it was a bust. Keith tripped on a rock and spilled all the plaster of paris, but there weren't any strange tracks to be found anyway. None that didn't match the treads on Alan's truck or his parents' vehicles."

"Did you take a look around Danica's house?"

"What for? Her driveway's gravel."

"Yeah, but there's a rutted path that goes past the end of the driveway around to the back of the house, remember? That's where I'd park if I was there to commit a major felony."

Roman sighed. "Okay, I'll try to check it out tomorrow morning before school. That all you wanted?"

"All for now," Jamie said with a wan smile, her

voice sounding choked by blocked nasal passages. "Get back to bed; you look like one of the walking dead."

"So do you." Roman blew her a kiss as he lowered the window, its descending screech as loud as the first. The barking dogs escalated their volume and tempo. Jamie hurried for the gate, hunched against the cold, thinking of nothing now but crawling into her own comfortable bed and cranking the electric blanket up to high.

When Jamie's alarm clock went off the following morning, she blindly groped for the OFF switch and silenced it, then promptly snuggled back under the covers, feeling completely miserable. Sometime after she'd finally crawled into bed someone had come along and exchanged her head for a snot-filled balloon. Her joints were achy and stiff and her forehead seemed hot enough to fry an egg on. There was no way she could make it through a day of school like this, and it was just as well. If she laid eyes on Morey Monroe again in a million years it would be too soon.

Her mother peeked in fifteen minutes later. "Jamie, you still in bed? It's past time to get up, dear. Come on, rise and shine."

"I'm not going to rise or shine," Jamie grumbled. "I'm sick. In fact I think I may be dying."

The door opened further and Gloria stepped into the room wearing an expression that was part concern, part suspicion. "What seems to be the matter?"

175

Jamie answered with a hacking cough and slurpy nasal inhalation which was enough to convince her mother that she wasn't faking illness just to get out of school. Not this time, anyway. Approaching the bed, Gloria placed cool fingers on Jamie's hot forehead and groaned sympathetically.

"You've definitely got a fever, and you sound just awful. How did this happen? You weren't sick at all yesterday. But you have been under a lot of stress lately. Guess it's finally taken its toll."

"Guess so," Jamie croaked.

"Well, all right, we'll keep you home today. I'll call the school and let them know. You rest now. Anything I can get for you?"

"A box of Kleenexes. And a priest."

Gloria patted Jamie's shoulder through the blankets. "I think you'll live. Not too many people die from the common cold."

But if any at all did, she would surely be one of them, Jamie thought dismally. Of course, she had no one to blame for this but herself and her stupid pride. The jerk would have given her a ride home if she'd kept her big mouth shut. No, that wouldn't have made any difference. Whenever she did something wrong and didn't get caught by her parents, God stepped in to dole out her just deserts.

Throughout the rest of the morning she drifted in and out of tortured sleep, escaping one nightmare only to drift right into another one. Around eleven her mother brought up some hot chicken noodle soup and told her that she had to go out for a short while, to do some shopping and keep a dental appointment at one. For an emergency Jamie could always call her father at the bank.

"Don't worry about me, I'm just gonna sleep," Jamie answered in her new stuffy voice, staring at the chicken soup with disdain. "Go on, I'll be okay."

As soon as her mother left the room, Jamie put the soup tray aside and pulled the covers back over her head. One moment she was burning up, perspiring like a sumo wrestler, the next chilled to the bone. By the time her mother's Cadillac backed out of the garage, Jamie was already fast asleep, her antibodies hard at war with the invading germs while her mind battled its own demons.

At some indefinable point in the timelessness of sleep came a bizarre dream in which she was in a cold operating room, on the table awaiting surgery, her prone body covered only by a white sheet. There were several unisex figures in the room with her, all wearing the standard baggy hospital greens, caps, and masks. They busied themselves doing God only knew what, something that involved a great deal of clanky metallic noises which made Jamie very nervous, as did all the secretive murmuring they did amongst themselves. She strained to hear what they were saying, but couldn't catch a word.

Then two heavy double doors burst inward and another one strode in, but from the air of importance (or arrogance) he/she/it exuded, Jamie guessed that the almighty surgeon had just entered. Stepping up to the table with gloved hands held upright, familiar green eyes fixed on Jamie's face. "Is everything ready?" A woman's voice, also familiar.

Frighteningly familiar.

Oh my God, Jamie thought. It's Miss Frupp.

She didn't stick around in the dream long enough to find out what type of surgery Miss Frupp was planning to perform. Probably a tongue-ectomy, if not a frontal lobotomy. She fought her way to consciousness, her only escape, and gradually became aware of her actual surroundings, the softness of her own bed, the feel of her fuzzy blankets, and the distinctive sound of the patio door in the den sliding open or closed. Very slowly.

Jamie's eyes flew open. Now she was fully awake, but a mere second ago she'd still been halfway between dreamland and planet Earth. Had she really heard what she thought she'd heard? It was hard to say. She lay very still, listening. All was quiet. Maybe her mother was back, and she'd gone through the sliding glass door to sit in one of the patio chairs with yet another drippy romance novel. But when Jamie looked at the clock to see how long she'd been asleep, she saw that it was only ten minutes past twelve. Much too early to have been her mother. So it was probably just her imagination.

Ditto for the slow creaking footsteps coming up the stairs.

Jamie bolted upright, panting through her mouth because both nasal passages were completely blocked. A few seconds passed in electrified silence, then she heard it again, another creak, softer, followed by another. It was not her imagination. Someone was definitely coming up those stairs. Jamie tried to convince her racing heart that it was her mother after all, that she'd canceled the dentist appointment and come home early, that she was creeping up the stairs so slowly, so stealthily, because she was trying hard not to awaken her. But her heart did not believe it, and kept right on racing.

Her heart believed it was Tommy Davidson. Even though she'd had suspicions about Morey Monroe, she found it impossible to believe that he would commit murder. It just couldn't be! Morey Monroe wouldn't be climbing up the stairs to her bedroom at this time of day. But Tommy Davidson, notorious Tommy Davidson, would.

And when he walked through that door, he would kill her.

In the space of a few pounding heartbeats Jamie's mind gave her a wide variety of options for self-preservation. Hurry and get under the bed. Hurry and hide in the closet (like you did in the nightmare—but he found you in there then, didn't he?) Hurry and jump out the window, so what if you break a few bones. Hurry and shut the door, but bummer—it doesn't have a lock! Hurry and find something heavy to clobber him with.

Or just hurry and say your prayers, girl, 'cause your ass is grass. She was too frozen by terror to do anything else.

But it wasn't Tommy who stepped into her open doorway. It was Morey Monroe. Jamie felt no relief—only surprise. Terror continued to hold her in its paralyzing grip. "What—what are you doing here?" she managed to get past her tightly constricted throat.

He stepped casually into her room, both hands shoved in the pockets of his baggy slacks. His eyes were everywhere but on her. "I feel really bad about last night, leaving you out there on the bridge. I couldn't wait for school to start so I could apologize, but you weren't there. So I cut out at lunch break and came over here to do it. I knocked several times, but didn't get an answer, so I thought maybe you were asleep or something."

Unable to stand it a moment longer, Jamie reached for a couple of Kleenexes and blew. "So you thought that gave you permission to break into the house?" Her voice quavered. "I seriously doubt my mom left any doors unlocked. Even if she's only planning to be gone for five or ten minutes she'll go back and check each one three times just to make sure. It's such a habit with her she does it even when my dad's here. By the way, he should be home any second now to check on me, and I don't think he'll be very pleased to find you here."

Jamie mentally patted herself on the shoulder

for her quick thinking. She didn't care if Morey had truly come to apologize for last night. She didn't trust him, and she wanted him out pronto.

His lips curled in a disquieting smile. "Oh yeah? It was my understanding that your dad had a twelve o'clock luncheon to attend, with a meeting afterward in which my father will be speaking on several important community issues."

"Don't worry, he'll manage to swing by," Jamie insisted in spite of the revealing blush she could feel creeping up her cheeks. She tossed the used Kleenexes into the trash can by her bed, hoping Morey didn't notice how shaky her hand was. "So I think you'd better leave. You've offered an apology, and I accept it. Everything's cool, okay? Now if you don't mind, I'd like to go back to sleep. I feel like hell."

Morey had meandered over to Jamie's dresser where he pulled his left hand from its pocket to touch and fondle the items haphazardly littering its surface: her earring tree and its dangling pairs of ornaments, perfume bottles, hair accessories, and makeup collection. His deliberate stalling was beginning to enrage her, and she didn't like him touching her things. Contrary to what she'd said, his apology had not been accepted and never would be. She'd only said that to get rid of him faster.

"Morey, if you stay in this room much longer you're going to get my cold."

Twisting her bottle of White Linen in circles, he gave her a sly sidelong glance. "But everything's not cool. I think you owe me an apology, too."

Jamie's mind balked. *She* owed *him* an apology? That was the most ludicrous thing she'd ever heard. Morey had to be the definition of arrogance. If she hadn't been so full of anger and fear, she would have laughed until she split a gut. "Excuse me, but would you mind telling me what for?"

Now he gave her a flinty stare. "For all that stuff you said about me. That I just use people like rungs on a ladder. Especially the part about God helping anyone who got in my way. Remember saying that, Jamie? It wasn't very nice, and I think you should say you're sorry."

In circumstances such as this, there was inevitably a point at which Jamie gave full reign to her emotions, instead of remaining within the guidelines of sanity and reason. Such as the next moment when she blurted, "You have the gall to talk to me about being nice? Everything I said is true."

He purposely knocked the perfume bottle over and stepped closer to the bed. "Is it? Guess it really doesn't matter, does it? What matters is what people believe. And they generally like to believe the worst of their fellow man, so they do. It makes them feel superior. Isn't that the real truth?"

"Not always," Jamie replied warily. "For instance, people don't get sent to prison on a judge or jury's whim. They make their decisions based on hard evidence, all prejudice laid aside. By the way, where did you go last Monday when you left the school at noon?"

Morey's face seemed to darken. "What's it to you?"

"Just curious. Did you go to the Dairy Queen like you said?"

"I don't see that it's any of your business," Morey retorted.

Just then Jamie's personal telephone rang. Both Jamie and Morey's eyes darted to the pink trimline on her nightstand. Jamie had never heard such a sweet sound in her life, although a worrisome thought arose that Morey would try to prevent her from answering it. "It's probably my dad," she said, reaching for the instrument as calmly as possible. Morey's expression turned decidedly stormy, but he didn't move to stop her, only told her in an intimidating tone not to tell the caller that he was there. He didn't want to get the mandatory week of detention for his unauthorized absence from the school property.

Jamie got a brief but nasty coughing fit out of the way, then lifted the receiver to her ear and said hello. It was Keith, but she hardly recognized his voice. It seemed lower, muted, and tight with tension.

"Jamie, I'm at Danica's house. Roman's with me. Erica's here, too, you know Danica's older sister from Houston. She's staying a couple of weeks. Anyway, me and Roman were just out back, checking around for tire tracks. There were some, but they'd been rained on and pretty much erased. Erica came out to ask what we were doing, and when we told her the truth, she got really upset and went back in the house. I'd noticed when she came out that she had a little book in her hand, but I didn't know what it was. Well, we were just getting ready to leave when she came running out of the house with that book again, which turned out to be Danica's diary. Erica had been reading it, thinking it would be okay since, well, you know. So she gets to the last page, and the last entry is dated September twenty-seventh, which was last Monday, the day you found her. Are you sitting down? Get ready for a shock."

Jamie threw a nervous glance up at Morey's face. He was standing over her like a vulture, his dark eyes boring into her with a cold, implacable intensity that none but a real vulture could match. *Say my name,* that look said, *and you're history.*

"Okay, I'm ready," she said uncertainly into the mouthpiece, not at all sure if she really was or not. Shocks were hardly ever pleasant.

A loud sigh was expelled in Jamie's ear, then Keith's voice—lower and even more tense—continued. "She was writing how she felt about giving her baby up for adoption, that it was going to be the hardest thing she'd ever do, but she knew it was the best solution. Then she stops right in the middle of a sentence and writes that there's somebody knocking on the back door, thinks it's probably you coming over to apologize. The next line says that she looked out the window and saw who it was. Jamie . . . it was Morey Monroe. And there's nothing after that; she never finished what she was writing about before. Seeing Morey on the back porch was the last thing she ever wrote."

Jamie felt her heart skip a beat. A giant danger alarm went off in her head, an explosion of shrill sirens and loudly clanging bells and swirling laser lights. The immutable facts were instantly presented in all their malevolent glory. Morey Monroe—not Tommy Davidson—had killed her best friend Danica. Sacrificed her life, and unknowingly, the life of her unborn baby, for extra votes in his father's pocket. That had to be as cold-blooded as they come. Subzero. Then, when rumors of Danica possibly being murdered began to surface, he planted the guitar pick he had taken from Danica's room on Tommy, the most logical scapegoat because of the threat he'd made on Danica's life. How convenient. Next he tried to recruit her to help him "find" it. Quite a nice bonus if he got to be one of the heroes. But Jamie didn't turn out to be a very cooperative puppet. Too bad for her.

Now Morey Monroe was standing not two feet away from her, and they were alone in the house. He had jimmied the patio door to get in.

And she was quite positive he had not come here to apologize.

Fighting to keep the fear out of her voice, she replied, "That sounds good, Dad, I'll tell Mom when she gets home . . . no, I don't need to see Dr. Purdom . . . it's just a cold, Dad, and besides, he's always got such bad breath it almost knocks you over."

Keith's voice came back, sounding worried. "Jamie, what's the deal? Are you delirious or is somebody else there?"

"Yes, I had some chicken noodle soup."

"Is it your mom?"

"No, Dad. Okay, I will. 'Bye." *Please, Keith, break the sound barrier getting over here,* Jamie prayed as she hung up the phone. She had to believe he was already on his way, blowing out the Hookers' front door like a hurricane, otherwise she'd start screaming her head off, which would surely clue Morey in that she was privy to his insidious secret. All she had to do was buy a little more time.

Morey folded his arms over his chest. "That was your dad, huh?"

Grabbing a few more Kleenexes from the floral-print box and honking into it, Jamie nodded, keeping her eyes averted from his withering gaze.

"Seemed he had a lot to say. What did he talk about?"

Come on, brain, you can do it. Jamie dropped the tissue in the trash with a moan of misery, hoping it effectively masked any overt sign of hysteria. "He called to tell me he was at that business luncheon for your dad; he'd forgotten all about it until his secretary reminded him late this morning. Told me what they were having and how

186

good it was, said he wants my mom to make it for dinner at least once a week." She shrugged. "That's about it."

Morey sneered, stepping a little closer as he slowly unfolded his arms. "You're so stupid. That luncheon was yesterday."

Jamie saw her life flash before her eyes. Her throat was seized by an invisible hand (or rope), making it almost impossible for her to breathe. Or speak. She couldn't do anything but stare back at Morey and know that he could see the stark terror in her eyes as if it were spelled out in neon.

Morey had begun clenching and unclenching his fists, a sure sign of the brutal violence to come. "You know, don't you? Or at least think you know. You haven't got a shred of proof. But the way you were talking last night, I got the feeling you'd figure it out sooner or later, or at the very least you'd go around shooting your mouth off, saying those same things about me all over town, turning people against both me and my dad, possibly losing him the election. No way can I let you do that." He paused as if waiting for a response, but Jamie remained mute, only fighting to pull air through the pinhole her windpipe had become. Her heart seemed to have stopped.

Morey inched closer to the bed until he was within half an inch of touching the blankets. Jamie could almost feel the waves of rage emanating from him, like heat waves off blacktop under a scorching July sun. "I notice you're not asking me what it is you're supposed to know, so that must mean I'm right. Who really called you on the phone? My guess would be one of your two good buddies, Manure King Keith Maguire or Girly Man Roman Alexander. You told them, didn't you? And I'll bet that's what the phone call was about, or you wouldn't have made up that bogus conversation. Of course, there was one other reason. To make them think something was wrong here, so they'd rush over to save you. Sorry to tell you this, but they *won't* get here in time, supposing they come at all."

Snarling like a wild beast, Morey leapt at Jamie and grabbed her by the throat. The terror that had been keeping her immobile instantly became the fuel for her survival. With a manic's strength she pried Morey's murderous hands from her throat and managed to roll him off her. He immediately fought to regain his hold, but in those scant moments she was able to lunge and grab the top half of the trimline on her nightstand and bring it down hard on Morey's head. She really was fighting for her life this time, and it was no-holds-barred. All was fair. If she could get to the gun — a .38 revolver — nestled beneath a pile of socks in her father's top dresser drawer, she would use it without hesitation, and she would aim for Morey's black, evil heart.

The handset greeted Morey's skull with a loud *thok*. Morey half roared, half yelled at full volume and instantly withdrew his hands from Jamie's throat to attend the injury, giving Jamie

188

just enough time and space to scramble off the bed and sprint for the open doorway. The best thing to do was just get out of the house, go screaming down the block for help. Morey wouldn't dare attack her outside in broad daylight. If she went for the gun, there was always the chance Morey would somehow get it away from her.

She'd just barely made it into the hallway when Morey tackled her from behind, sending them both sprawling to the floor. Jamie screamed, kicking and flailing for all her muscles were worth. During the fierce struggle that ensued, her mind was ravaged by images of her own body hanging from a rope, her face purpled and swollen as Danica's had been. She saw herself laid out in a casket, too, made to look in peaceful repose, surrounded by flowers, being gazed upon by her horrified parents. Then her mind blanked as Morey again succeeded in getting his hands around her throat, his thumbs pressing savagely down on her windpipe, effectively cutting off her air supply. She could feel a terrifying tingling sensation in her head, a sure sign that she was very close to blacking out. Spots appeared before her eyes as she fought back in a wild frenzy, gagging, screaming in her mind loud enough for the whole planet to hear. But she was losing; the blackness was quickly creeping in, stealing her consciousness and her life. But with one last desperate burst of energy, she rather accidentally got a good knee shot into Morey's groin.

Apparently the pain was too intense for vocal expression. His face screwed up in a caricature of agony and he doubled over, yanking his hands from Jamie's throat and cupping them together in the crux. Gulping much-needed air into her lungs, Jamie would've liked very much to take a picture of him in such deserved agony, but this was her cue to get scarce in a hurry. Jerking her legs out from under him, she stumbled backward to her feet, then tried to sprint past him for the stairway, but one of Morey's hands shot out and grabbed her by the ankle, causing Jamie to fall facefirst onto the carpet.

"Give it up, Jamie!" Morey bellowed with a demon's voice, vehement and steeped in hatred. "Today's your day! Don'cha wanna be up there in Heaven with your friend Danica? Don't you miss her?"

Jamie clutched at the carpet, hyperventilating, dangerously close to breaking down in tears, which would undoubtedly leech away the rest of her strength. "You've got a big problem you don't know about yet," she snarled at him between clenched teeth, her voice sounding whiskey-rough due to her bruised larynx. "We do have proof. It may be a little on the circumstantial side, but it would sure make a jury think. Last Monday you told practically the whole cafeteria that you were going to the Dairy Queen for lunch. But you didn't go there, and Nancy Leibelle will swear to it. So where did you go? Well, as it so happens, Danica was writing in her diary when you showed up at her house to kill her. She wrote down in her diary that she saw you standing out there on the back porch. And that is, as they say, all she wrote. Add to that the fact that you're a total fanatic about your father's political career, and that you knew about the blood pact me and my friends — which included Danica — had made, threatening to kill ourselves if the old depot was torn down. What a setup, huh? Of course there was no guarantee things would go your way, people turning against the mayor over that, but they sure did, didn't they? Everything worked out just perfect. Except for one little hitch. If Keith's not on his way over here, he's on his way to the sheriff's office with that diary. *You* give it up, Morey. This just *isn't* your day."

Jamie could hardly believe what happened next. Morey the coldblooded killer actually broke into elephant tears, sobbing like a child, blubbering a string of unintelligible words. He released his grip on her ankle and pushed himself into a sitting position, drawing his legs up and hanging his face between his knees, his hands clasped over his head. "I just wanted . . . I just wanted . . ." was all Jamie was able to understand.

She almost felt sorry for him. Almost. She thought him still capable of great cruelty. Mainly she felt relieved that it was over, and that it hadn't cost another life. Which reminded her. "What about Alan?" she asked with forced gentleness. "Did you try to kill him too?"

"No," Morey responded sulkily. "Just Danica."

191

Just Danica.

"Not just Danica," Jamie corrected, wanting him to bear all the guilt to which he was entitled. "She was pregnant. You killed her baby, too." She was left to wonder if Alan really had tried to do himself in, or if it had been a drinking-related accident, or if it had been a Tommy Davidson-related incident. Solving that mystery was next on her list.

After a moment of stunned silence, Morey lapsed back into racking sobs. With a sigh, Jamie rose to her feet and shuffled tiredly back into her room to call the sheriff. Replacing the handset in its cradle to get a dial tone, she trumpeted a sneeze, then an unexpected smile touched her lips. Woo-wee, was the *Deer Creek Review* going to have a heyday with Sheriff Hammond's gross incompetence. With a little help from her friends, Jamie had succeeded in wrangling a confession out of the culprit that Hammond had insisted did not even exist. And it felt good. Real good.

She had just started to dial when she heard a loud squeal of tires in front of the house. Moving closer to the window she saw Keith's pickup parked half on the street, half on the lawn, the driver's door hanging open. A second later the doorbell began ringing insistently. Jamie was suddenly aware of how terrible she looked, and to top it off she was wearing her dorkiest pair of pajamas again. But Keith was obviously extremely worried about her, so she'd better go answer the door before he did something rash and heroic like break a window or try to knock down the door. She hung up the phone and hurried out of her room, skirting the defeated, weeping ball of humanity in the hallway on her way to the stairs, which she galloped down two at a time.

When she unlocked and opened the front door, a very-frantic-looking Keith gaped back at her. "I thought you were in some kind of trouble."

"I was," Jamie said grimly, stepping aside to let him enter. Lowering her voice to a near whisper she added, "Morey's upstairs. He broke in while I was asleep to kill me. I might be dead if you hadn't called, but with the information you gave me I was able to bring him to his senses. Where's Roman?"

"Sheriff's office with Erica. They were going to show Hammond the diary and demand that he issue a warrant for Morey's arrest."

Jamie glanced toward the staircase. "Let's just go ahead and take Morey over there, special delivery. He won't give us any trouble; he's nothing but a big baby at the moment. But I need to get dressed first. Wait here, in case he tries to sneak out while I'm in my bedroom."

Keith gave her a dazed look and nodded.

Chapter Ten

Sheriff Hank Hammond slammed his meaty fist down on his green metal desk, toppling over a full pencil holder. His face was almost crimson with anger. "Dang-blast it, I've heard enough! And I'm hungry! Now get outta here with this so-called evidence of yours and let me go on to the cafe afore my stomach starts eatin' itself!"

Roman stared down at Danica's diary, lying open on Hammond's leather-framed blotter. On the yellowed paper around it elaborate doodles were drawn, some in ink, some in pencil. So this was what the sheriff did when he wasn't feeding his voracious appetite, Roman thought. Once upon a time there must have been an ad for sheriff in the *Deer Creek Review* that said: Wanted, fat slob who could eat a Mormon out of house and home and make interesting doodle designs. IQs of 60 or above need not apply.

He started to tell Hammond that he was going to go over his turnip of a head to the attorney general's office with Danica's diary — he wasn't at all sure that was the right place to go, but it sounded impressive—but before he could get out the first word, the front door burst open and Jamie strode in like she owned the place, head held high, shoulders back, hands on her hips. She was followed by a meek, red-eyed Morey Monroe who kept his eyes glued to his shuffling shoes. Keith brought up the rear, looking like he'd just lost a few marbles and was trying to figure out where they'd gone.

Nudging Roman aside to stand directly in front of Hammond, Jamie pointed a steady finger at Morey Monroe. "Arrest that person, and book him on murder one. He murdered Danica Hooker and tried to kill me fifteen minutes ago."

Hammond's face turned a slightly darker shade of crimson. "How about I arrest you for kidnapping? You think you can just up and haul anybody in here when you feel like it? Whaja do, beat 'im up first? That there's assault and battery."

Jamie thought someone should arrest Hammond and charge him with impersonating a higher primate. She turned to Morey. "Tell him."

"I did it," Morey mumbled obediently.

A startled look claimed Hammond's porky features. "What? Speak up, boy!"

For the first time since entering the sheriff's office, Morey slowly lifted his eyes, pausing a few seconds on the open diary before meeting Hammond's disbelieving stare. "I did it, I'm guilty," he said loud and clear in a weepy voice. "I killed

Danica Hooker. I tried to kill Jamie. But you know what, Hammond? I'm only confessing because I know there's no way a whole jury could be as stupid as you. But I haven't been read my rights yet, so I'm still eligible for a plea bargain."

Slowly but surely the angry coloring in Hammond's face faded to a pasty white. "Good God."

Danica's sister, Erica, standing apart in her own embrace, quietly began to cry.

"I guess we'll leave him in your capable hands now," Jamie said sarcastically to Hammond. "And remember, that diary is an important piece of evidence in the case against Mr. Monroe here, so don't lose it or mistake it for a sandwich and eat it. And one more thing, Sheriff Hammond." She paused to sneeze. "I'd advise you to start learning a new trade, because after I earn my college degree in criminology or law enforcement, I'm coming back here to run for sheriff. I think it's about time Deer Creek had a real one."

Leaving everyone speechless, she turned and marched out.

In the wake of Morey Monroe's arrest for murder came three significant events. The first was Malcolm Monroe's anticipated withdrawal from the race for mayor and from society in general. This triggered the second event, Mayor Shepherd's happy announcement to the effect that he'd had a change of heart concerning the old railroad depot. He would let it stand, and use the money earmarked for the statue, benches, and gardens to refurbish the public library—which didn't win him many points, but with Monroe out of the way, he was running unopposed again and it really didn't matter if anyone liked it or not. The third event was Jamie's full pardon from being grounded and losing her car keys. It had seemed difficult for her father to say it, so programmed was he to dish out only disparaging remarks where Jamie was concerned, but he told her that he was proud of her. He also said the idea of her running for sheriff completely horrified him (that was distinctly a *man's* job!) but he wouldn't stand in her way, if that's what she really wanted to do. At least she now had the gumption to go to college, make something of herself other than a permanent slave to menial jobs and minimum wages.

The following Saturday evening Jamie took great care with her clothes and makeup, wanting to look as attractive as possible for Keith when he came by to pick her up at seven. The mayor's plan to tear the old depot down had been canceled, but the party planned by the older teens had not. Jamie still had her cold, but a time-release analgesic and a couple of aspirin had relieved most of the symptoms.

Keith's pickup pulled up front five minutes early. Jamie called out to her parents in the kitchen that she was leaving, and hurried out before her mother could appear with some hideous head scarf for her to wear.

Keith smiled broadly when she got in. "Got a

call while ago from Alan's mother. He's come out of his coma, and the doctors say he's going to pull through."

"God, what a relief," Jamie said, smiling herself. Then she suddenly turned serious. "Do you know if he's talked to anybody about what happened?" At school on Friday they'd tried bluffing Tommy into a confession and had gotten nowhere.

Nodding, his smile also fading, Keith put the transmission in drive and pulled away from the curb. "He did it, he tried to kill himself. Decided he was worthless, just a scab on the butt of society. Couldn't take listening to his parents at each other's throat anymore and didn't think there was any other way out. And he thought Danica had done it, which made him think of it as kind of a challenge."

Jamie stared blankly at her clasped hands, shaking her head. "He needs help."

"Yeah, and he's going to get it. His mom told me all three of them are going to get whatever treatment or counseling is necessary. Speaking for Alan's dad as well as herself, she said this experience was like getting hit in the face with a bucket of ice-cold water. They know how close they came to losing their only son, and it scared the hell out of them. Literally."

"Shame it had to go that far," Jamie said. "But I'm glad to hear they're going to work at straightening things out."

When they pulled up in the flattened brown

198

grass near the depot, she was surprised to see they were the first ones there. Hot on the heels of her surprise came a giddy nervousness about being alone with Keith at the number-one make-out spot in Deer Creek. Since her crush on Morey had been thoroughly and permanently extinguished, she'd been secretly considering the impossible possibilities again, this time with a more open mind, taking Keith out of normal context, but always backing blushfully away from these thoughts in fear her brain waves might get picked up by the local radio or television station.

"Looks like we're the early birds," Keith said, shutting off the pickup's noisy engine. Its rattle was immediately replaced by the chirping symphony of countless crickets.

After a long silence, which Jamie began to imagine was charged with intimate tension—the strength of his desire to take her in his arms and give her a French kiss she'd never forget—Keith turned to her and said, "You wanna play Rock-Scissors-Paper?"

Jamie stared at him at moment, then gave way to a rising fountain of laughter that was surely born of relief. "Sure, Keith. Why not?"

SCREAM
Skin-prickling stories of horror
that will keep you screaming
for more!

Next . . .
THE DEAD GIRL
by Jo Gibson
(Coming in November 1993)

It was amazing the way Julie Forrester resembled her cousin Vicki. She could have practically passed for her twin! Too bad Vicki isn't alive anymore, having tragically died in a car crash. But even though she's dead, Vicki is still a part of Julie's new life in Colorado. Everywhere Julie goes, she's mistaken for her dead cousin. Soon strange and terrifying events start to happen and Julie starts to realize someone unknown thinks she's Vicki.

And that someone wants her dead.

Please turn the page for an exciting preview of THE DEAD GIRL

One by one, the skating party broke up. Ross escorted the guests back to the lodge, Donna and Paul went home to get ready for work, Gina left with Dave, and Julie found herself alone on the ice. She thought about going back to the lodge, too, but it was a perfect opportunity to practice her skating. No one would see her if she fell down, and she certainly wouldn't bump into another skater since she was the only one on the rink.

The music was still playing, and Julie took one last turn around the rink. She was definitely gaining in self-confidence, and she didn't even wobble as she glided across the ice. Then the music stopped. Someone must have shut it off up at the lodge. Julie skated in a tight circle in the center of the rink, and watched the purple shadows lengthen on the face of the mountains.

The air was lovely, crisp but not cold, and her winter parka kept her toasty warm. The sun was a huge golden ball, almost touching the peak of the mountains, and mountain blue jays called raucously from the pine trees bordering the far end of the rink. Julie stopped to listen, standing on one skate and balancing with the toe of the other. And then she heard it. The snapping of a dry pine branch, the rustle of a body crashing through the trees.

A deer? An elk? A bear! Julie's eyes swept the edge of the wooded area, and she saw something moving near the base of a large pine. Then she blinked and the shape was gone. Perhaps it had been one of the lodge cats. Aunt Caroline kept several strays to keep down the mice population.

One more lap, and she would go back to the lodge. Julie began to skate again. The blades on her skates made soft, shushing sounds against the ice, and she smiled as she fell into an easy rhythm. As she glided past the far end of the rink, she felt an uneasy prickling at the back of her neck. Eyes were watching her. From the trees.

"Hello?" Julie's voice was shaking as she called out. Perhaps one of her classmates had forgotten something and was coming back to get it. "Is anyone there?"

But there was only silence. Silence and the sensation of breathing, back in the pines where the shadows were deepest. Someone was there. Julie was sure of it. And that someone was watching her!

Suddenly the sun dropped behind the mountain peak and darkness began to fall. She'd forgotten how quickly light faded up here in the mountains. Julie's breath came in ragged gasps as she pushed off from the rail and raced toward the warming house. There was barely enough light to see. And someone was watching her! Waiting for darkness to fall!

Her fingers fumbled frantically with the laces and she pulled off her skates as fast as she could. Where was he? Out there somewhere, waiting for her to come out? But she couldn't stay here. She had to get back to the safety of the lodge!

Then she heard footsteps, coming across the ice, straight toward the warming house in a direct path. Heavy footsteps. A man's footsteps!

Julie dropped to her knees and scuttled under the wooden bench. Her heart was beating so hard, she was sure he could hear it. He knew she was in here. And now he was coming to get her!

Then the footsteps paused, right next to the warming house. "Julie? Are you still here?"

Lights blazed inside the warming house, and Julie blinked in confusion. Ross's voice. Ross was here.

"I'm just . . . uh . . . putting on my boots." Julie slid out quickly and plunked herself up on the bench. There was no way she'd let Ross Connors catch her acting like a terrified child!

Almost immediately, Ross stuck his head around the corner. "Sorry, Julie. I would have turned on the lights sooner, but I thought you came in."

"No . . . I decided to skate a little longer."

"Are you all right?" Ross looked worried.

"I'm fine. And I'm ready to go." Julie pulled on her boots and stood up. "Ross? Were you standing out there by the pine trees?"

Ross shook his head. "I came from the other side of the woods. Why?"

"I . . . uh . . . I just thought I heard something in the trees, that's all."

"And it scared you?"

Ross gave an amused chuckle, and Julie quickly shook her head. "No, not at all. I was just curious."

"Well, it was probably a raccoon. They get pretty hungry this time of year, and they start coming up to the lodge at dusk. That's why we keep our garbage in the shed."

Julie nodded and smiled. "Of course. A raccoon. I should have known."

Ross took her skates and slung them over his shoulder. As they started walking up the trail to the lodge, Julie considered it. No, not a raccoon. And not any other type of animal, either. She was sure that a man had watched her from the shadow of the pine tree. And whoever he was, he'd intended to scare her!

Julie dressed in a red and black plaid skirt and a cheery red sweater, and brushed her long blond hair until it was shining. She pulled it back with a red velvet ribbon, and glanced at the clock on her dresser. It was almost six, and she'd told Aunt Caroline she'd be downstairs at six-thirty to handle the switchboard.

Since she was early, Julie took the elevator to the lobby and walked through the deserted restaurant to the small, private dining room. One wall was glass and it had a lovely view of the snow-covered grounds which were lighted at night with low spotlights. The other walls were wood-paneled, and there was a huge stone fireplace with a portrait of the founders of the lodge, Julie's great-great-grandparents, hanging over it.

Julie walked over to the long table that was set up in the middle of the room, surrounded by twenty red leather chairs. Ten standing ice buckets were lined up nearby, champagne chilling in each of them. Julie recognized the distinctive label. Dom Pérignon. This must be a very important dinner party. She'd noticed that Dom Pérignon was the most expensive champagne on the menu, over a hundred dollars a bottle!

There was a smile on Julie's face as she glanced at the table itself. Three bouquets of fresh flowers had been arranged on the white linen cloth, red roses peeking out from lacy white baby's breath and delicate green ferns. Aunt Caroline had told Julie she'd taken a class in flower arrangement so she could do the centerpieces for the tables.

Silver gleamed and crystal wineglasses sparkled under the soft glow from the recessed lighting overhead. And to add a touch of warmth and comfort, someone had started a cheery blaze in the stone fireplace.

"Nice, huh?" Donna came in, carrying a stack of china plates. "We always go all out for one of Mr. Stratford's parties. You never know who might be coming. I've waited on senators, and movie stars, and a bunch of millionaires. Of, course none of them bring their wives."

"Why not?"

"Dick Stratford supplies the women."

"Dick? That's short for Richard, isn't it?"

Julie frowned as Donna nodded. Another "R." There were so many, she'd have to start keeping a list. Ross, "Rock," Ryan, Richard Stratford, Red Dawson, and even Uncle Bob, since his name was Robert!

"Dick Stratford's got a whole phone book full of gorgeous young girls." Donna looked amused. "And they all want to be invited to one of his parties. You'll see what I mean when they get here."

Julie nodded. She should have guessed. Ryan was smooth, and he'd obviously had plenty of practice with his father's women. "What does Mr. Stratford do?"

"You mean besides drink, and sleep with gorgeous women, and throw money away?"

Julie laughed. "Yes. What does he do for work?"

"He doesn't. Oh, he flies to New York every week or so to check on his magazine, but that's it."

"Which magazine?"

"*Fantasy.* Have you heard of *Playboy,* or *Penthouse?*"

Julie nodded. "Of course. Mr. Stratford's magazine is like that?"

"Sort of. Except it has less articles. Paul's got a stack of them under his bed, and it's mostly just pictures of naked girls."

"And those are the girls Mr. Stratford brings to his parties?"

"You got it." Donna began putting out the plates. "At least he doesn't bring them in naked. Mrs. Hudson wouldn't let him. They're dressed. . . . but barely."

Julie raised her eyebrows. "Who's helping you serve tonight?"

"Mrs. Larkin. Your aunt won't let the boys work Mr. Stratford's dinners anymore."

Donna was grinning, and Julie had to ask. "Why not?"

"Because Paul dropped a whole bowl of creamed spinach last year, when he recognized

September's top model."

The two girls burst into laughter, but they quickly sobered when Julie's uncle came into the room. He was frowning.

"Isn't that table set yet?"

"It's almost ready, Mr. Hudson. All I've got left are the water glasses."

Donna set out the rest of the plates and hurried back to the kitchen. The moment she was gone, Uncle Bob turned to face Julie sternly. "Don't bother Donna when she's working. She's slow enough as it is."

"Yes, Uncle Bob." Julie's eyes flashed with protest, and she quickly dropped her gaze. Donna wasn't slow. Aunt Caroline had said she was the best waitress at the lodge.

"I need you on the switchboard, Julie. One of our guests wants to place a call to France."

"All right, Uncle Bob." Julie turned and hurried to the lobby. There was something wrong with Uncle Bob tonight. He was just as crabby as the day she'd arrived, and this time there were no German guests to frustrate him.

It took only a few moments to place the call. Julie spoke to the international operator in English and the Paris operator in French. At least her foreign language skills were helpful. Uncle Bob couldn't complain that she wasn't pulling her weight, here at the lodge. But he wasn't the type to thank her or even give her a compliment. Uncle Bob was a gruff man.

Julie had just finished answering several reservation calls, when Donna rushed into the lobby. She looked up with a smile as Donna darted around the back of the desk and set down a small plate.

"Louisiana Crab Cakes. They're our special appetizer tonight. But don't let your uncle see them. He doesn't let anybody eat at the desk."

"Thanks." Julie moved a piece of paper over to hide the plate. "What's wrong with Uncle Bob tonight? He's really crabby."

Donna moved closer and lowered her voice. "I think he's drinking again. He went on a real bender after Vicki died, and he hasn't been the same since. Talk to you later, Julie. I've got to run."

Julie stared after Donna as she hurried back into the restaurant. She thought she'd smelled liquor on Uncle Bob's breath this afternoon, but she hadn't been sure. And Donna's comment had just jogged loose another unpleasant memory of Aunt Caroline's visit.

On Aunt Caroline's last night in Tokyo, her mother had put her to bed early. The grownups had wanted to talk. But it had been too early for Julie to sleep. She'd climbed out of bed and opened her door, padding down the hallway on silent, bare feet. That was when she'd heard her aunt crying.

"I just don't know what to do. He doesn't come home until late, and when he does, he's

been drinking. And I'm almost sure he's been seeing another woman. He's cheating on me. And he's an alcoholic! What kind of father is that for Vicki?"

Julie's mother had sounded very sympathetic. *"Maybe you should divorce him, Caro."*

"I can't! You know Mom and Dad didn't want me to marry him in the first place. I just can't bear to admit they were right!"

Julie's father had cleared his throat. *"If you won't get out of the situation, Caro, you have to think of some way to change it. Can you get him to go to A.A.?"*

"Maybe. I know he doesn't want a divorce. He loves that lodge like it's his own. He's always wanted to run it."

"That's it, then." Julie's mother had sounded very sure. *"Tell him you'll divorce him if he doesn't get some help. And don't back down."*

"How about the other woman? I'm sure he's seeing someone."

Julie had peeked around the corner and watched her father put his arm around Aunt Caroline. *"A.A. might help with that, too. Just take it day by day, Caro. And if it doesn't work out, come straight back here to us."*

Julie had watched and listened for a while longer, but she'd been too young to understand what was happening. She'd known that everyone was upset, and that had made her upset, too. She'd gone back to her bed and snuggled up

212

with her favorite stuffed toy for comfort, and then she'd fallen asleep. And when she'd awakened the next morning, Aunt Caroline had gone back to America.

This sudden flash of memory was very insightful. Julie had wondered why her aunt waved the wine bottle away at dinner, and now she knew. Uncle Bob was an alcoholic. That was why the liquor cabinet in their living room was filled with nothing but soft drinks. And it also explained why Uncle Bob had been so crabby. If he was drinking again, he was probably feeling very guilty about his lapse.

Just then the front door opened and a crowd of people came in. One glance at them and Julie knew exactly who they were. The men looked rich and successful, and they were dressed in expensive casual wear. And the women were exactly as Donna had described. And then some! The last time Julie had seen so much bare skin was on a nude beach in the South of France.

The women were young and beautiful. Their hair was perfect, their makeup was faultless, and they were all smiling up at their dates with identical adoring expressions on their faces. They were dressed in low-cut evening gowns, and, to use the new slang phrase Donna had taught her, they all had bodies to die for. Julie thought they looked like they didn't have a brain among them, but they were gorgeous.

The man in the lead was dressed in slacks

and a black silk shirt, open at the neck. His jacket was slung casually over his shoulder, and he looked like he'd stepped right out of the pages of a men's fashion advertisement. He had dark curly hair and a deeply tanned face. Julie recognized him immediately, and she drew in her breath sharply. This had to be Dick Stratford. His eyes were the same shade of slate gray as Ryan's.

He strode toward the desk, the walk of a man who knew exactly where he was going and why. But he stopped cold as he saw Julie.

"Mr. Stratford?" Julie smiled and her heart beat a little faster. His eyes were every bit as compelling as his son's.

"Yes." His voice was deep and intimate, and Julie shivered. It was a bedroom voice, a voice that would whisper sweet, sexy things in some lucky woman's ear. He stared at Julie, blinked hard, and then he smiled. "Ah, yes. The little cousin. Julie, isn't it?"

"Yes, sir." Julie took a deep breath. "Your table is ready. If you'll wait just a moment, I'll call for the hostess to show you the way."

"That's not necessary, honey. We've been here before. Come on, Bambi. Let's go." Dick Stratford tucked his date's hand under his arm, and escorted her toward the private dining room.

Julie stifled a giggle as she watched them leave. Dick Stratford's date was aptly named. She had long honey-colored hair and huge brown eyes with impossibly long eyelashes. Her lips were pouty, her walk was a sexy wiggle, and her legs were long and coltish under a white silk dress slit up both sides. It was lucky that Paul was no longer allowed to work at one of Dick Stratford's parties. If he'd seen Bambi, he would have dropped much more than a bowl of creamed spinach.

After Dick Stratford's party had left to go into the dining room, there was a flurry of calls. Julie answered them quickly, connecting one to the housekeeping desk, another to the long-distance operator, and a third and fourth to room service. Mixed in with the in-house calls were several requests for reservations, and one inquiry about a tour group which she referred to Ross.

The old adage was true. After the storm came the calm. There was a long, silent interval when the phone didn't ring at all. Julie listened to the sounds from the dining room, glasses clinking, silverware clattering, the low hum of polite conversation. That got boring after a while, and she'd just opened her history book to do a little extra reading when the phone rang again.

"Saddlepeak Lodge. This is Julie speaking. How may I help you?"

There was silence and Julie frowned. A bad connection? She could hear noise in the background and a crackle of static, but the sounds were faraway and indistinct. She was about to hang up, when she heard a muffled voice.

"Julie. You look so pretty in that bright red sweater. Don't do what your wicked cousin did or you'll wind up dead, too."

Then there was nothing but silence again, and the faint indistinct noise in the background. Julie shuddered, and her fingers gripped the receiver so tightly, her knuckles turned white.

"Hello? Hello? Who is this?"

But there was no answer, just the faint crackling of a bad connection. And then she heard something that frightened her even more. A low chuckle that grew to an ominous laugh. And then a click. And a dial tone, loud and jarring, as the call was cut off.

The phone slipped from Julie's nerveless fingers and dropped back into the cradle with a thump. A wrong number? He'd known her name, but she'd identified herself when she'd answered the phone. It could have been a prank, a childish attempt to scare her. But why? What had she done to make someone want to frighten her?

She sat behind the desk, face white, hands shaking, trying to imagine why anyone would make such a call. The voice had been deep and gruff. A man's voice. He'd known that she was Vicki's cousin, but everyone in Crest Ridge knew that.

Julie reached out for a piece of paper and forced her shaking fingers to write down the words exactly as he'd spoken them. *Julie. You look so pretty in that bright red sweater.*

She was about to continue when she looked down at the bright red sleeve of her sweater. The pen dropped from her shaking fingers and she gasped in terror. He'd known what she was wearing! Her caller was here, and he was watching her!

Julie felt the back of her neck prickle. It was the same feeling she'd had at the skating rink, the feeling of being watched by hostile eyes. She swiveled around to stare out the window. The grounds looked lovely and peaceful, a white expanse of freshly fallen snow that glittered under the spotlights. Perfectly beautiful. Perfectly still. But he could be out there somewhere, peering out from the corner of a building, or hiding behind one of the huge pine trees. He could be anywhere, lurking in any of a thousand dark shadows while she sat here shaking, pinned down by the switchboard, exposed by the bright lobby lights.

Deliberately, Julie turned her back on the window. She told herself there was nothing out there, no reason to be in such a panic. She'd been sitting at the switchboard for over an hour and there had been a steady stream of guests and employees who had walked through the lobby. Any one of them might have noticed that she was wearing a red sweater. It was only a prank. A mean, spiteful trick. She should ignore it, and go on as if it had never happened.

Although Julie did her best to push down her fear, nothing she tried had any effect. She could still hear the echoes of that muffled voice, and with each passing second, her anxiety grew. Her heart pounded hard and adrenaline surged through her veins. Her mind was flashing a message to her trembling body. Scream. Run to the safety of the restaurant. But how would she explain why she'd left the switchboard? Uncle Bob would think she was crazy to get so upset over a crank phone call.

She had to write down the rest of the message. Julie picked up the pen again, and forced herself to continue. *Don't do what your wicked cousin did or you'll wind up dead, too.* The words were ominous and she stared down at them as if they could somehow magically explain themselves. *Wicked* was a strange word to use, almost old-fashioned, the type of word you'd hear in a fairy tale. How had Vicki been wicked? What had she done?

Julie pushed that part of the sentence out of her mind and concentrated on the rest. As she read the words, she felt her panic rise to the surface again. At first she'd thought that Vicki's death was accidental. That was horrible enough, but then Donna had told her that Vicki had committed suicide, something Julie found even more dreadful. This message hinted at something even more frightening, something so gruesome Julie didn't even want to think about it. Vicki had been wicked, and now she was dead. What if Vicki hadn't committed suicide? What if she'd been murdered?

Julie shuddered as she remembered that chilling laugh. And the creepy feeling of being watched. If the man on the phone had murdered Vicki, would he try to kill her, too!

LOOK FOR *THE DEAD GIRL* ON SALE AT BOOKSTORES EVERYWHERE IN NOVEMBER 1993!

WHEN YOU HAVE GIRL FRIENDS —
YOU HAVE IT ALL!

Follow the trials, triumph, and awesome adventures of five special girls that have become fast friends in spite of — or because of their differences!

Janis Sandifer-Wayne,	a peace-loving, vegetarian veteran of protests and causes.
Stephanie Ling,	the hard-working oldest daughter of a single parent.
Natalie Bell,	Los Angeles refugee and street-smart child of an inter-racial marriage.
Cassandra Taylor,	Natalie's cousin and the sophisticated daughter of an upper-middle class African-American family.
Maria Torres,	a beautiful cheerleader who's the apple of her conservative parent's eye.

They're all juniors at Seven Pines High. And they're doing things their own way — together!

GIRLFRIENDS #1: DRAW THE LINE (4350, $3.50)
by Nicole Grey

GIRLFRIENDS #2: DO THE RIGHT THING (4351, $3.50)
by Nicole Grey

GIRLFRIENDS #3: DEAL ME OUT (4352, $3.50)
by Nicole Grey

SUSPENSE IS A HEARTBEAT AWAY —
Curl up with these Gothic gems.

THE PRECIOUS PEARLS OF CABOT HALL   (3754, $3.99/$4.99)
by Peggy Darty
Recently orphaned Kathleen O'Malley is overjoyed to discover her long-lost relatives. Uncertain of their reception, she poses as a writer's assistant and returns to her ancestral home. Her harmless masquerade hurls Kathleen into a web of danger and intrigue. Something sinister is invading Cabot Hall, and even her handsome cousin Luke can't protect her from its deadly pull. Kathleen must discover its source, even if it means losing her love . . . and her life.

BLACKMADDIE   (3805, $3.99/$4.99)
by Jean Innes
Summoned to Scotland by her ailing grandfather, Charlotte Brodie is surprised to find a family filled with resentment and spite. Dismissing her drugged drink and shredded dresses as petty pranks, she soon discovers that these malicious acts are just the first links in a chain of evil. Midnight chanting echoes through the halls of her family estate, and a curse cast centuries ago threatens to rob Charlotte of her sanity and her birth right.

DARK CRIES OF GRAY OAKS   (3759, $3.99/$4.99)
by Lee Karr
Brianna Anderson was grateful for her position as companion to Cassie Danzel, a mentally ill seventeen year old. Cassie seemed to be the model patient: quiet, passive, obedient. But Dr. Gavin Rodene knew that Cassie's tormented mind held a shocking secret—one that her family would silence at any cost. As Brianna tries to unlock the terrors that have gripped Cassie's soul, will she fall victim to its spell?

THE HAUNTED HEIRESS OF WYNDCLIFFE
MANOR   (3911, $3.99/$4.99)
by Beverly C. Warren
Orphaned in a train wreck, "Jane" is raised by a family of poor coal miners. She is haunted, however, by fleeting memories and shadowy images. After escaping the mines and traveling across England with a band of gypsies, she meets the man who reveals her true identity. She is Jennifer Hardwicke, heiress of Wyndcliffe Manor, but danger and doom await before she can reclaim her inheritance.

WHITE ROSES OF BRAMBLEDENE   (3700, $3.99/$4.99)
by Joyce C. Ware
Delicate Violet Grayson is hesitant about the weekend house party. Two years earlier, her dearest friend mysteriously died during a similar gathering. Despite the high spirits of old companions and the flattering attention of charismatic Rafael Taliaferro, her apprehension grows. Tension throbs in the air, and the housekeeper's whispered warnings fuel Violet's mounting terror. Violet is not imagining things . . . she is in deadly peril.

Available wherever paperbacks are sold, or order direct from the Publisher. Send cover price plus 50¢ per copy for mailing and handling to Zebra Books, Dept. 4355, 475 Park Avenue South, New York, N.Y. 10016. Residents of New York and Tennessee must send sales tax. DO NOT SEND CASH. For a free Zebra/Pinnacle catalog please write to the above address.